an imprint of Amplify Publishing Group

www.mascotbooks.com

The Secret of the Kelimutu Volcano: The Rise of Golden Garuda

For more information, please contact:
Mascot Kids, an imprint of Amplify Publishing Group
620 Herndon Parkway, Suite 220
Herndon, VA 20170
info@mascotbooks.com

Library of Congress Control Number: 2023914219

CPSIA Code: PRV1023A
ISBN-13: 978-1-63755-938-3

Printed in the United States

To my family: my mom and dad, my husband, my lovely daughters, and my sister.

I would also like to dedicate this book to my sources of inspiration: the smiles of Indonesian children. They are a reminder of the good in the world, the simple pleasures in life, and a hope for our future.

THE SECRET OF THE KELIMUTU VOLCANO
THE RISE OF GOLDEN GARUDA

HAMSA BUVARAGHAN
RIYA SANJAY & EESHA SANJAY

Dear Annmarie,

Enjoy reading!

Love,

Hamaa. B

THE CURSE

THE DAY AISHA WAS BORN, Kelimutu—which had been dormant for ages—erupted, causing devastating damage to her village. To Aisha, it was not a coincidence. And, in fact, a wise magician had prophesized that it would happen again when she turned ten. Her birthday was just a week away.

Aisha slouched over, neck bent, legs close together. She twisted her hands, then placed her right fist to her lips and closed her eyes. Perhaps she'd brought a curse upon her town . . . What else could explain the last eruption and this terrifying prophecy? The townspeople of Moni shunned her. *But what could she do?* Her stomach churned. She really wanted to save Moni and her people. If the curse was her fault, at least she could be the one to make everything right.

She opened the curtains and peeked out of her window at Kelimutu. Craggy cliffs, stones, and boulders dotted the landscape while low-hanging clouds covered the mountaintops in mist.

Aisha lived on remote Flores Island in Indonesia, close to Kelimutu Volcano and the lakes in Nusa Tenggara Timur. The island scenery varied from low-land savannah to volcanic rainforest. Red-flowered flame trees between the palms made the view spectacular.

The waterfall near her home, which had always been a source of calm and comfort, today sounded like a thunderous battle, its water pounding the rocks with relentless ferocity. The hair on the back of Aisha's neck stood up, her palms sweated, and her entire body began to tremble.

She watched as her mother, Zaha, flipped the living room calendar to June 6, 1956—one month before her tenth birthday. The day was marked with a drawing of two girls trekking to Kelimutu. Why had she agreed to this? Liya, her eight-year-old sister, could be so persuasive; there'd be no getting out of it now.

"Aisha, you must get over your fear," said her mother. "Go ahead on the trek you promised your sister. It will be fun for the two of you to visit the crater lakes. When I was your age, I was always outside exploring the mountains."

Just then Aisha's grandmother, Dewi, walked in. "I can attest to that. Your mother was outdoors all the time."

"Grandma," said Liya, pointing to the drawing of the two girls trekking. "I'm going on the trek today with Aisha to Kelimutu and the crater lakes."

"Liya is too young to go there alone. As a big sister, you need to go along," said Grandma. "You have to see with your eyes how the three mysterious crater lakes of Kelimutu change color."

"I wonder what color the lakes are this time," said Liya.

Aisha recalled that last time when Grandma took Liya there, lake Tiwu Ata Mbupu was white, that the lake Tiwu Nua Muri Kooh Tai was green, and that the lake Tiwu Ata Polo—the enchanted lake—was red. Aisha had heard her whole life about how the lakes were spectacular. She was willing to take their word for it.

Grandma said, "I have seen many earthquakes and volcanic eruptions in my lifetime. The color of the crater lakes at any time is a direct reflection of the great force. Whenever the dark power grows stronger, the lakes will turn brown, and this is when Kelimutu will rumble and roar, devastating everything in its way.

"The day you were born, Aisha, Kelimutu did not spare anyone in its path. The forests were destroyed, the trees were burnt, all the houses were wiped out, and the townsfolk had to rebuild the entire town. Next time it will be even more devastating. There is nowhere to go, and we will all surely die."

Zaha threw her hands up in frustration and said, "Ma, you're just scaring Aisha even more."

Aisha wished she could do something, but she was so scared

and so alone in that fear. She was the only one in all of Moni who refused to climb Kelimutu's slopes. Liya often climbed Kelimutu, accompanied by either her mother or grandmother, going to the crater lakes, but no matter how many times she suggested that Aisha come with her, she never did. The crater lakes were very special to Liya; she had even discovered her special powers there.

Liya had inherited her mother's magical gift, the ability to heal any living creature with a touch. Everyone in Moni admired them, but Aisha was a bit jealous of her little sister.

"I can't find it," cried Liya, frantically looking through the contents of the bookshelf. As she was clumsily searching, she knocked a pile of books to the living room floor. Finally, turning to a chest of drawers, she pulled out a map made from dried palm leaves that they had woven together. Aisha and Liya had painted Kelimutu and labeled and colored the many different paths that led to its peak.

Liya ran and retrieved a knapsack with all the things they would need to climb the slopes. Liya had been trying to persuade Aisha to join her and had been packing supplies into the special knapsack for the last six months. By this point, it was very heavy.

"That won't work." Aisha laughed. "You have too many things in there. It is too heavy to carry up the slopes."

Liya dropped the bag and it burst open, revealing twenty

different items she thought they needed for the trip, including a rope, a collapsible handheld telescope, a spyglass, a flute, a conch for signaling an emergency, and games—like *Kelereng*, which was a game of marbles, and *lompat tali*, which was a jump rope.

"This has everything except food. With your appetite, it will be twice the weight after you pack that." Aisha laughed again, feeling better. She loved Liya dearly, as her sister's silly innocence always melted away her worries.

The living room floor was quite a mess now. Aisha helped Liya put everything back in the knapsack. She helped her clean up and neatly stack the pile of books back on the shelf.

Once they were done, Liya pulled Aisha by the hand, forcing her out of the house. It was a beautiful summer morning; the air smelled fresh, and the early birds were chirping. It was the first week of their summer break from school.

Reluctantly, Aisha joined Liya on the trek to Kelimutu. From Moni it was about six miles to get to the base of the volcano. They walked to the nearest bus stop. Within minutes the bus arrived. The sisters boarded the small twelve-seater bus. Aisha chose an empty seat next to the window and Liya sat next to her. The bus passed through several green paddy fields and then made a few winding turns. After they finally passed the river, it came to a complete stop at the Kelimutu parking lot, which was at the base of the volcano.

Aisha and Liya started on the hike, ascending the steep slopes. The peak of Kelimutu looked like it was studded with the tips of sharp arrows. From what she had learnt from Liya, it would take them at least thirty minutes to get to the top of the mountain. She could do it, as it was just half an hour away. She tried hard not to be afraid. Her legs trembled like leaves in a storm, and her breath came in ragged gasps. She looked toward the top of Kelimutu. She had to overcome her fear, but could she do it? Her little sister had already done this so many times. She glanced up and saw that Liya was already way ahead of her. Meanwhile, Aisha's stomach churned, and she broke into a cold sweat. The early morning rays of the sun that should have felt warm were instead like cuts to her skin. Pain stabbed her head and she felt faint.

Without a second thought, Aisha darted back down the slopes.

"Aisha, don't be a coward," Liya called out. Without heeding Liya's words, she ran downhill as fast as she could, profusely sweating and panting. As she reached the base of Kelimutu, she frantically looked around for buses at the parking lot. One bus was heading toward her home, so she jumped aboard, tears rolling down her cheeks. She folded her knees up on the seat and bent her head over her lap, hoping that no one would see her crying. When the bus driver announced her stop, she got down, wiped her eyes with her sleeves, and ran to her house. She fell flat on the living room floor as soon as she had let herself inside.

Grandma Dewi sat down next to Aisha. "You are shivering with fear, my child," she said. "Aisha, my girl, do you see what is happening? Your fear is taking over you." Somehow, her grandma always understood her; she was the only one who could save her from her pathetic situation.

"You don't need to feel so hopeless," said Grandma. "Soon, my child, you will conquer your fear and uncover your true calling. Listen to the voice within you, for it will guide you to your destiny. Do not compare yourself with your little sister. You don't need magical powers to be special."

Aisha wasn't so sure about that. She was the only one in her family with no magical powers—a cursed child. *Would she discover her destiny? Perhaps her tenth birthday would be the time to find out.*

Later that day when Liya had returned from Kelimutu, Aisha walked over to Grandma's house, the biggest in her village. Grandma was one of the oldest and the wisest in the town, and the oldest person in the village always stayed in the biggest house. Its roof was made of thatched *alang-alang*—blady grass—and soared high, looking like a curved cone. The house had a square layout. Four main posts supported the house. Grandma always said that these posts were imbued with mystic symbolism.

She stood outside and peeked into the small openings in the wall, which was made of plaited palm boughs. She loved looking through the small windows; she would often make strange animal sounds to startle Grandma. She loved playing pranks on her grandma. As she was thinking about what prank she'd play next, a noise caught her off guard.

Someone pounced on her from behind. Aisha spun around in a panic, only to burst into laughter. It was only Liya trying to scare her. She felt embarrassed to have chickened out of the trek, leaving her sister alone. Luckily, Liya didn't bring it up. Aisha chased Liya around Grandma's house, and it wasn't until later she realized she'd forgotten all about her fears of the curse.

Suddenly Aisha heard a chatter of voices and a roaring engine. She turned back to see what was happening.

THE BAJAUS

Across the shore of the beach about fifteen yards from Aisha's home, several strangers were speaking in high voices, but she could hardly understand what they were saying. Her grandmother muttered something and pulled Aisha inside the house.

Moni was a hidden paradise, and no outsiders ever came to their island. Aisha peeked from the window and saw five boats at the shore: several small canoes and one large plank boat with a sail. Several groups of women, men, and children were getting off the boats. Some of the men held fishing poles and carried several small bags. They looked like they were fishermen or sailors.

"Bajau people," announced Aisha's grandmother. "The Sea Wanderers have arrived, and they will soon bring misfortune and spells with them."

"Who are the Bajaus?" asked Liya. "What misfortune and spells?"

Grandma looked at Liya. "I hope they don't settle down here," she said in a whiny, high-pitched tone.

Aisha peeked outside through the window and pointed to the strangers. "Look, Grandma, the Bajau men are already putting up tents."

The Bajau children had bright eyes, and their skin was bronze in color. They had big smiles on their faces. The women wore colorful red and yellow skirts. Aisha saw one old Bajau man who was slightly hunchbacked and walking with a big stick. He had gray hair, and his face was time-worn and wrinkled. He had a somewhat crooked, pointy nose and a distinctive beard that was straggly and unkempt.

As Aisha was peering through the window, the old Bajau man suddenly looked directly at her. Aisha shrieked and closed the window, for he had piercing eyes. She ran and hugged her grandmother.

"Why did the Bajaus choose our village?" Aisha asked. "How long will they be here? Are they bringing trouble?"

"I don't know what is happening," said Grandma. "All I can tell you is stay away from them. Do you hear me? *Stay away from them!* Their actions will only make the dark power grow stronger."

Outside, someone began to play beautiful music. Then Zaha walked into Grandma's house.

"There must be a really talented musician in the midst of

this new Bajau tribe," her mother said. "We should see who is playing."

Aisha hurriedly pulled her mother's hand. "Mama, don't go out. Don't talk to them. Grandma thinks they can bring misfortune."

Mother laughed and turned toward Grandma. "Ma, not all Bajaus are bad. I know you are concerned about what happened last time, but this is a new tribe, and they have so many young children. We must welcome them. After all they are only staying for a little while."

Aisha heaved a big sigh of relief at these words. She held her mother's hand as they walked outside.

Women and men hurried around, trying to pitch tents. A row of five had already been put up. The cloth on the tent was tattered in many places and randomly patched up with different colored scraps of material. She saw some young babies crying, and she watched as their mothers rocked them while simultaneously trying to repair their new homes. A girl who looked about the same age as Aisha waved at her. Her clothes were torn, and she looked like she really needed a bath. She held a ragged doll and looked very cheerful despite her circumstances. Aisha waved back to her. The Bajau girl ran to the old, hunchbacked man. Aisha wondered if they were related. Should she stay away from the girl?

Suddenly Aisha heard the same music from earlier. A

middle-aged man with curly black hair was sitting on a rock and playing a *rebab*, a bow fiddle. Aisha couldn't believe the beautiful sound it made, very much like the red bird-of-paradise that twittered on the branch at the back of her house. He seemed to be the only one in the group unbothered, not caring much about settling down or putting up his tent. His music was so soothing that Aisha felt her mood almost instantly change.

When his song was finished, he stood up and began playing a more vibrant song with a faster tempo. Many kids gathered around him, holding hands and swaying and dancing to the music. Aisha was curious to find out more about these strangers and looked up at her mother.

"Go on, Aisha," her mother said, understanding the unspoken question. "Join the other children."

With her mother's approval, Aisha went over to the Bajau children. At first, she stood still, paying attention to the different dance steps and observing everyone's movements. She then joined them, slowly getting the hang of the folk-dance moves. Feeling confident and comfortable among the Bajaus, Aisha called out to Liya to join her. They held hands and danced.

The music's pace picked up. Aisha struggled to dance even faster, laughing and giggling with other children and making mistakes and correcting them along the way. Aisha and Liya were soon thoroughly enjoying themselves. A Bajau girl came toward Aisha and took her hand, pulling her to dance. Aisha obliged. After all, this was her only chance to make a new friend who didn't know anything about her cursed background. She demonstrated a few new dance moves, and Aisha meekly followed her. Almost another hour of dancing and giggling followed. By this time, Aisha had befriended the Bajau girl, Shelta.

"This was so much fun," said Aisha loudly to her mother after the music stopped. *The Bajaus don't seem so bad.* On the contrary, they seemed so much fun. Aisha made her way home with her sister, all the while watching over her shoulder.

THE VOLCANO

THE NEXT DAY, AISHA WOKE up to the stench of rotten eggs.

"What is that horrid smell?"

"That is sulfur, Aisha," her mother said. "The volcano next to Kelimutu had a short eruption last night when we were asleep. Nothing to fear."

Aisha rushed out of the house to check on Kelimutu. She did not see anything coming from the volcano, but the air was thick with smoke and the foul sulfur smell.

She rushed back inside and immediately closed all the windows, then peeked through one of them and watched the Bajaus heading back from the smoky mountains. They had tied scarves around their noses and mouths, probably to escape the sulfur. They danced and jumped, sometimes throwing their hands into the air. As they reached the bottom of the mountain, they removed the scarves from their faces, and Aisha saw that they were beaming. They talked and laughed loudly, looking excited to have found something. Each of them was carrying a small bag, which they kept looking into and showing each other the contents. One woman dropped her bag, revealing many shiny crystals.

"Ma, come to the window! Look, beautiful crystals have dropped from the bag," said Aisha.

"What an irresponsible thing to do, going after gems, especially close to an active volcano," her mother said.

Aisha's grandmother walked into their house and joined them at the window. "Seems like our new neighbors are fascinated by crystals, and they want to collect them even if it means risking their lives."

"What do they do with the gems, Grandma?"

"They use them to make jewelry that they can sell. They also secretly hope that they might stumble upon some magical crystals," said Grandma.

"How do they find these gems, Ma?"

"When the volcano erupts," her mother explained, "hot molten lava flows out. When this cools down, it releases dissolved minerals and creates colorful gemstones. As Grandma said, Bajaus collect these gemstones in the hope of selling them. Sometimes they collect them thinking it will bring them good luck."

"Beware of the Bajaus!" Grandma Dewi added. "They also steal crystals and gems."

Aisha moved closer to her mother, touching the amethyst

necklace that she always wore. "Will they steal your necklace?"

"There is nothing to worry about, Aisha," her mother responded and glared at Grandma. "Ma, not again. Bajaus don't steal. You should stop saying this. You're planting all these misconceptions in the minds of my daughters. You know how strongly I disagree with you about this."

Zaha's eyebrows were lowered and drawn together in a *V*. She walked out of the house without saying another word. Aisha followed her mother. Her mother got distracted as a patient stopped to talk to her. Aisha walked out further, leaving her mother behind. She saw strong glares from the villagers and a group of town children were talking in hushed tones. She walked toward them, and one small girl yelled, "Go away, cursed child! Leave Moni! I don't want to die. I don't want Kelimutu to erupt." Aisha's eyes swelled up in tears.

The little girl was right. She was cursed. *How could a cursed child like her ever save Moni?* She should leave the town. Her presence was putting everyone in danger. Sadly, she headed toward her house.

As she was turning back to return home, something caught her eye. From somewhere, an eagle swooped in front of her. Suddenly she saw a very bright light flashing as the eagle flew up in the sky. *Was that a golden hue?* thought Aisha as she looked up.

EAGLE CIRCLE

SEVERAL EAGLES WERE SWOOPING INTO the town. They perched at the top of different trees, some glancing deeply to identify any easy prey, some just ruffling their feathers. There must have been over ten or so bald eagles. They all let out a cry, each one of them—a distinct shrieking cry. First, they were separate cries one after another, then the clouds grew dark and then there was a chorus of shrill cries from all the bald eagles. As this grew louder and louder, more eagles swooped in the sky. Now there were hundreds of them.

Hundreds of bald eagles descended from the dark clouds, circling around the town, filling the village with screeching cries. The eagles were everywhere, perched on top of the trees, above the rooftops of houses, flying and circling above the lake. It was a crazy sight. It was a huge congregation of eagles, indeed.

When the eagles spotted their prey, they launched from their perch in the trees and landed perfectly on their prey, dragging it to the shore to feed. The salmon and smaller fish were swimming as fast as they could, but alas they were not swift enough for the vicious predator. Their destiny was imminent.

Villagers ran out of their homes to see the mad congregation. Bajaus came out of their tents trying to shoo the eagles. There was no stopping this scene. The shrill cries continued despite the attempts from the Bajaus until most of the fish on the lake were eaten by the hungry eagles. The Bajaus must have lost their entire catch for a month. There were no more fish left.

And then from the sky rose a golden hue resembling a giant ball of fire. It grew bigger and bigger until the whole town lit up in piercing sharp light. One had to look away. Aisha looked through the glaring haze of light, and what she saw she could just not comprehend.

A golden giant eagle with a crown on his head was flapping its giant wings in perfect harmony. Half-eagle, half-human, he rose in the sky. He grew and grew until he was as big as the sun swooping over the town with red wings and a yellowish golden face. He flew straight to the top of the Kelimutu volcano. He did not look smaller as he flew further and further. Instead, he looked the same size, although he was very far away from the town. And then a clang of bells filled the air, Garuda—the eagle-man—stood over the top of Kelimutu with his hands over his hips. He stood there tall and looked over, moving his eagle face to either side as if inspecting the village. By this time all the villagers had run into their homes in fear. For some strange reason, Aisha could not take her eyes off Garuda.

The giant eagle soared through the air, his golden crown slipping from the head and tumbling to the ground below. Then, with a high-pitched shrill, he swooped down in front of her. Aisha felt a pleasant warmth from him. Garuda took his hands and gently touched Aisha's head. "You will be rid of all fear now, my child," said Garuda. Before Aisha could say anything, he flew into the clouds.

THE VILLAGE HEALER

AISHA WENT HOME. SHE WANTED to tell her mother about Garuda, but her mother was busy mixing health potions in the kitchen. There was a patient seated in the room waiting for her. Aisha watched her mother. She was so beautiful, with dark-brown eyes and a prominent nose. Her long and lovely black hair was unbound, and her neck was always adorned with her precious amethyst necklace.

Everyone respected her mother. After all, she was the village healer, a doctor. When anyone had health concerns, they came to consult Aisha's mother, who always seemed to know what they needed. Aisha marveled at how her mother balanced family with her duties as a healer. She hardly had any time to rest, so Aisha loved to help out. Over the years, she had seen her mother heal many patients that came to their door. She was the epitome of compassion. She was able to know what was wrong with every patient, and she was a very competent healer. Every time Aisha saw a patient thanking her mother,

her heart swelled up with pride.

Most of the herbs her mother used grew in the mountains and plains around where they lived. Aisha could identify a few by sight, as well as their healing properties. Crushed mint leaves helped with digestion. Applying peeled turmeric root on a wound helped it heal. She observed her mother as she measured carefully and made the various potions, every now and then pushing back her long, black hair.

With the doors unlocked, her house was a beacon of hope for the sick and injured. If anyone was in need, Aisha's mother would immediately help them. Being a healer was a very respected position and had been so for generations. Grandma was also a great healer, and Aisha's mother often went to her to consult a set of palm-leaf manuscripts inscribed with medicinal knowledge to treat different ailments and diseases. These manuscripts were kept apart from their home in a small shed with all the finished potions and hanging herbs.

Aisha's mother was preparing to receive her patients that morning when a knock rattled the door. Aisha got up to open it. A patient, a woman she didn't recognize, stood on the top step. She covered her mouth as she coughed. Aisha asked her to come inside and have a seat.

Aisha's mother walked up to her and held her wrist to feel for her pulse. She asked the patient to open her mouth and shone a small flashlight inside. She then asked Aisha to bring her ginger, scallions, and brown sugar. Aisha took the needed items and handed them to her mother. She watched as her mother took a few scallion stalks and sliced ginger and cut it into ten small pieces. After setting a pot of water to boil, her mother added the ginger, scallions, and a little brown sugar and let it all simmer.

Aisha noticed that her mother's amethyst necklace was glowing as she worked.

"Drink this warm potion three times daily, and you will be better," said Zaha as she poured the health potion into the two bottles and sealed them.

Aisha looked at her mother's necklace again. It had that strange glow whenever her mother tended to her patients. Her eyes had a similar glow when she focused on making medicines. Liya got that glow in her eyes as well. Her mother and sister were both very special indeed, very talented healers like her grandmother. But why not her?

When her mother had finished with her patient, Aisha sat on her lap and touched the amethyst necklace. "Mama, this crystal always glows when you are healing. Tell me about this necklace. I'm big enough to know, since I will be ten next month," insisted Aisha. She knew she was bringing up a subject that her mother always kept secret from her.

"I'm wearing a very precious amethyst, a protective stone symbolizing power and courage. It also gives me the power to focus my energy on those in need. This necklace should never land in the wrong hands," said her mother.

Aisha nodded, but her curiosity was aroused. *Could the amethyst have anything to do with her mother's healing magic? Did her mother also give Liya a secret stone? Why does Liya have the same healing magic?* Alas! She was the only one in her family with no special powers. What was the story behind the amethyst necklace? How did her mother get it? She had to find out. Perhaps a magical stone could also give her some powers . . .

All Aisha knew was that Grandma had mentioned one time that it had been given as a gift when Mother was very young. *Perhaps Grandma will tell me the story.*

GRANDMA'S SECRET

Determined to find out the truth, Aisha ran over to her grandmother's house across the street. Grandma always had answers. She opened the door and hugged Aisha. "Come in, my dear, I see your curious expression. What is troubling this little head?" she asked, stroking Aisha's hair. Grandma's touch was always comforting, her hands were soft and smooth, and she had a warm heart.

"I want to know more about how Mother got the amethyst necklace. Tell me, Grandma, who gave it to Mama and why?" asked Aisha, following Grandma into her kitchen as she was removing a pan from a cupboard and setting it to heat.

Grandma always made *martabak manis*—sweet crepes— when Aisha went to her house.

"Your mother wears a *kecubung* stone," said Grandma while she added the batter to the pan. "She considers it very special. She thinks it has special powers and removes negative energy. Your mother also believes that her healing powers are enhanced when she wears the amethyst."

"Patients *are* calmer after they see Mama," Aisha said.

"Zaha is a great doctor and healer, much better than me, and she has cured so many people in this town with her healing powers—but the stone is not magical. Your mother is naïve to believe it has powers. After all, it was given to her by a Bajau."

"A Bajau granted Mama this gift?" asked Aisha.

"Yes, before I moved to this town, I lived near *Gunung Egon*, Mount Egon."

"Was Mount Egon as huge as Kelimutu?" asked Aisha, just as Grandma brought her a plate with a sweet crepe.

"Mount Egon was a volcano located in the southeastern part of Flores, near Maumere Bay," said Grandma. "One day, we had a massive volcanic eruption. A large cloud of ash and smoke came from Mount Egon."

"How old was Mama then?" asked Aisha, munching her food.

"Your mother was ten years old," said Grandma. "The eruption caused an ash plume to rise more than ten thousand feet above the volcano's crater. It caused a very heavy landslide, and many homes were swept into the ocean. I left all my possessions behind. I just grabbed your mother's hand, and we started running.

"Now, when I think of that terrible day, I can't believe we are even alive. All my neighbors and the people in the town, about a hundred people, were swept into the ocean. When the landslide quieted down, I stopped to look back. I heard a feeble cry from afar. I walked with Zaha toward the cry, and the cry got louder as we got closer to the ocean. That was when I saw a small baby, frantically crying. The baby had been swept away by the terrible landslide into the ocean. It was floating in a basket all alone."

"Oh! Poor baby!" exclaimed Aisha.

"I saw that baby floating in the waves, and I heard its ear-piercing cry," said Grandma. "Since the landslide had subsided, I took your mother to a flat area and made her sit. I jumped into the ocean with just one hope: to save the helpless baby."

"What happened?" asked Aisha, sitting upright.

"I swam until I reached the baby. I grabbed the basket and swam back to shore," said Grandma. "The baby was very cold. I had to make sure she was alive."

"What did you do then?" asked Aisha.

"I placed the baby on her back on the firm ground. I gently tilted her head back with one hand and lifted her chin with the other. I put my ear to the child's mouth and nose and tried to listen and feel for signs that she was breathing."

"Was the baby alive?" Aisha asked out of concern.

"I could not hear breathing," said Grandma, "so I placed my mouth over the baby girl's nose and lips, and I gave two breaths, each lasting about a second. Then I noticed her chest rising and falling. I felt for a pulse—the baby girl was fine! She was breathing."

Aisha clapped. "You saved the baby. Grandma, I'm so proud of you, you are so brave!" Aisha hugged and kissed her grandma in excitement, even though of course she understood this had happened decades before she was even born.

"As Zaha and I tended to the baby, two people ran toward us frantically: a woman who was about my age with her young son. She looked like she had lost everything. She was the baby's mother, and the boy was about twelve years old with a strange moon-shaped scar on his cheek. He wore a black stone earring in his left ear. They were Bajaus."

"They must have been so relieved to see the baby safe," said Aisha.

"Yes, the mother ran and held the baby girl, thanking me profusely. She really wanted to give me something in return," said Grandma. "She pulled out an amethyst and thrust it into Zaha's hand."

"The amethyst is from the Bajau mother, then?" asked Aisha.

"Yes, it must have been something they stole. It has no magic. It's nothing but a stolen gem. I have been trying to tell your mother this for so many years. Alas, she does not listen to me," said Grandma, looking frustrated and angry.

"But, Grandma, I have seen it glow many times," said Aisha.

"Are you saying that I'm lying?" asked Grandma.

Aisha said nothing; she did not want to upset Grandma.

It was better she stayed quiet, knowing there were several sore points between Mother and Grandma. She would hate to provoke any more tension.

"Run along now," said Grandma. "I don't have any more to tell you."

Aisha was disappointed, as she'd hoped to learn more from Grandma. She had seen the amethyst shine bright so many times so there had to be more to the story than what Grandma was telling her.

Aisha walked home, dejected that she had not gotten the full story behind the amethyst. She went straight to her mother. "Mama, do you remember the woman who gave you the amethyst?"

"How do you know it was a woman?" her mother asked.

"I asked Grandma."

"I see, my little girl is getting very curious," her mother said with a laugh. "I don't remember what she looked like, but I do believe it is magical. When she handed me the amethyst, she said it had special healing powers, and I know it does."

"Grandma didn't say that, even though I asked her."

"I faintly recall the woman who gave me the amethyst. There was one small thing that made me uncomfortable," her mother said. "As she was giving me the amethyst, her son yelled and grabbed her hand to stop her. He seemed very angry when she ignored him. And after she handed me the amethyst, they walked away, and I never saw them again."

Why had the boy been so upset, and why hadn't he wanted his mother to part with the amethyst?

THE BIG DAY

AISHA WENT TO BED EARLY, lying in bed thinking through what her mother and grandmother had told her about the amethyst. Not long later, she glanced out of the window right next to her bed and saw a strange woman in a green robe, with long, slightly curly black hair cascading down her back. Her fingers were slim, and she had long nails. She looked hazy, as if she was somehow part of the fog outside. Who was this woman? She didn't look like anyone in their town. Then, to Aisha's surprise, the woman called to her: "Aisha, follow me." Aisha was intrigued: how did she know her name? She tried to speak but no words came out of her mouth.

The strange woman was luring her. Aisha tried to hold on to the blankets, but her fingers were loosening their grip. Aisha got up as if drawn to her by a magnetic force and blindly followed her, leaving the house and slowly making her way toward the peak of Kelimutu until they reached a statue of a giant bird. It looked like a statue of Garuda, the giant eagle bird, and it was wearing a crown.

"There are four impressions on the crown, Aisha. You need to find the four mysterious gems," said the woman, glancing at her with bewitching eyes. "There is no time to lose. Put them on this crown. Only then can you suppress the dark power and stop the volcano."

"How will I know where to find the stones?" asked Aisha, finally forcing words out of her mouth.

"I will guide you, and the voice inside you will take you. Every stone is unique, and you will know when you see it. You are this town's true savior, Aisha. You are the chosen one!"

"Why me?" asked Aisha.

There was no answer, and the strange woman only disappeared into the green fog.

Where am I going to find these mysterious gems? Who is this woman? How can I save the town when I brought the curse upon Moni?

Suddenly, a huge monster rose from Kelimutu. It had long teeth, sharp claws, and menacing eyes. The monster grew and grew in size until Aisha could hardly see the face. It came toward Aisha.

"Mama, Mama," cried Aisha as she screamed and sat up in bed.

Her mother ran into her room.

On seeing her face so pallid, she said, "You look as if you have seen a ghost. What happened? A bad dream?"

Aisha wiped her clammy hands on her blanket to rid them of sweat. No words came out of her mouth. Her chest was pounding.

Seeing her shaking uncontrollably, her mother sat beside her in the bed and gave her a warm hug.

"There is nothing to fear. It must have been a nightmare." Her mother kissed her on her forehead and tucked her back into bed. "It's still very early. Go back to sleep. Think happy thoughts, for tomorrow is a very special day."

But Aisha still couldn't fall back to sleep. Instead, she thought about the dream as she lay in bed. She tossed and turned. Was it time for her to climb up Kelimutu? Was it the answer to all her questions? Was the dream a calling? All of a sudden, the thought of Kelimutu did not give her any anxiety; instead she was intrigued. Had the strange woman cast a spell on her? Why? She didn't feel afraid anymore.

Aisha made a resolution: she had to climb Kelimutu. It was about time.

Her thoughts were broken when her mother and Liya came into her room. "Happy birthday, Aisha!"

Her mother gave her a hug, and Liya gave her a big, tight squeeze as well.

"Happy birthday, Aisha!" yelled Liya, jumping for joy and

raising her hands in the air.

That morning was indeed special. It was Aisha's tenth birthday. "Liya, I will go to the top of Kelimutu with you today!" said Aisha, much to her sister's surprise.

Liya could hardly contain her excitement. She babbled on about how she was going to show Aisha where she had discovered her secret powers.

Aisha rushed to the kitchen. Their mother was preparing a sumptuous breakfast of *nasi goreng*, fried rice with vegetables. Mama always believed in a very big breakfast, and as today was her birthday, the breakfast was extra special. The aromatic fragrance of the cooked *nasi goreng* filled the air.

"I can already tell the *nasi goreng* is going to be extra yummy today," said Aisha as she looked at the huge cooking pots and sniffed the air. She looked inside the other big pan.

"Why are you also making *mie goreng*?" asked Aisha. *Mie goreng* was Aisha's favorite fried noodle dish.

"You can eat the *nasi goreng* now, and I am packing the *mie goreng* for you and your sister. It looks like today is going to be a long day for you two. I want to make sure you don't get hungry."

Aisha smiled, feeling even more determined with her mother's support. She hugged her tightly. Her mother reminded them that they had to ascend the slopes before sunrise.

Aisha and Liya quickly got dressed.

Aisha could hardly believe that she had finally decided to climb the slopes of Kelimutu Volcano. What fear she had lived in, blaming herself for the past eruption, scared of the prophecy. The dream evoked a newfound confidence in her, to break away from any fear and to seek her destiny. It was time for her to discover what secrets lurked in Kelimutu.

Their mother checked Liya's knapsack one more time for all the important items—map, whistle, the *mie goreng*, and snacks.

With perfect timing, Grandma walked in. She hugged Aisha and kissed her on her head. "Happy birthday, Aisha. I see you are ready with the knapsack again. Today is very special, my dear. Just follow your instincts and believe in yourself. Your destiny is inside you. You have everything it takes." Grandma touched Aisha's chest.

"Look outside," Aisha's mother said. "Kelimutu is so calm. It is waiting for you. Be brave, Aisha, and you will discover your destiny."

She kissed both girls, and the sisters waved goodbye to their family and set off on their journey.

Aisha held Liya's hand and walked outside. She smelled the fresh air. There was no lingering smell of sulfur. It seemed like a perfect day to climb Kelimutu.

As they climbed, Aisha sang the destiny song her grandma had taught her.

Your destiny always awaits you.
Your destiny is always inside you.
Do you have the courage?
Do you have the readiness
to seek what you need to seek,
to give what you need to give?
Your destiny always awaits you.
It is up to you to find it.
Only you can truly feel it.
No one can teach you.
No one can help you.
It is your journey.
The journey awaits.
Your destiny always awaits you.

THE GREEN MIRAGE

THE SUN WAS RISING, AND as they walked up the slopes of Kelimutu, the hike got steeper and steeper. Aisha felt like a very different person: someone with no fear and no past inhibitions about Kelimutu. She thoroughly enjoyed the hike. They took a detour to get to the small peak where they could get the best view of the sunrise and the crater lakes as their mother had suggested. They slowly hiked through big crags and boulders up to the small peak and sat down on a big rock.

"This is a great spot to watch the sunrise. What a great way to start my birthday!" exclaimed Aisha. The girls fell silent as the sun rose, mesmerized by the view of the first rays of sun, the three crater lakes, the color of the clouds, and the spectacular view.

"Liya, now I understand why you always wanted me to come here. I really want to go to the crater lakes now. If they look so beautiful from afar, I wonder how they will look when we go closer," said Aisha, breaking the silence.

They had their morning snack of *martabak* and felt very energetic. They continued to climb up, sometimes running, sometimes walking, sometimes chasing each other. Aisha laughed and giggled, making jokes with her sister, until they reached their final destination—the mysterious crater lakes.

"See now, we are up at the crater lakes!" Liya said. "This is Tiwu Nua Muri Kooh Tai, the first lake."

"Wow! The water is so crystal clear. I can see the bottom," said Aisha.

Aisha knelt down, and as she dipped her hands in the water, her fingers tingled as if chilled. The moment her hand touched the water, the entire lake turned a brilliant shade of green, similar to the fresh leaves of the trees.

"What have I done?" Aisha asked, backing away. Her eyes filled with tears. "My touch must have contaminated the water." She ran away from the lake sobbing bitterly.

"Come back, Aisha! There is nothing to fear, sister."

Aisha walked back to the lake. The water was green but still clear. The color had not had any effect on the aquatic life, and fish were swimming as before. The only difference was the green hue.

Aisha looked closely at something glittering: a shiny rock in the water. There were slight steam fumes coming out near the rock. Heat trails drifted up from the bubbling water.

"Be careful, there are several hot springs here," warned Liya, as she'd been here so many times before. Aisha felt pathetic; although she was the younger sister, Liya had much more experience on these mountain peaks than she did. She had to step up as a big sister. Perhaps she could start this very moment. Taking a deep breath, Aisha walked over to the hot springs. She heard the burble of water as it was heating up and watched as the bubbles pushed to the surface. The air was filled with the smell of sulfur and damp rock.

"Watch out, Liya. Don't go too close to it," said Aisha, holding her back. Aisha crept closer and used a short stick to try to move a shiny rock, but it seemed stuck.

"We need something stronger to pull that," she said. "Liya, see if you can find a longer, thicker stick. I will need two sticks to scoop this out."

Liya looked around and then reached for her knapsack, in which she'd packed a sturdy stick. "Here, see if this works."

Carefully, Aisha used the two sticks to pick up the gleaming stone. As she was nearing the surface of the water, the gleaming stone flew up straight into the air, followed by a wisp of green smoke.

"No, no, no, this is not happening!" said Aisha as she looked up. Liya's eyes were wide open, the white showing the whole iris. She stared without blinking.

Was that green vapor coming from the stone? thought Aisha. It created an image in the air as if the stone was drawing something.

"Are you seeing what I'm seeing?" asked Aisha. "It looks like a woman with a green robe. She has long hair and is holding something. I'm certain I've seen her before." Aisha scratched the back of her head, trying hard to remember. She shook her head in frustration; she could not recall anything.

Suddenly she felt the hair on her body rise and a chill ran up her spine. "She's holding a gleaming green stone."

"She's calling you," said Liya in a high-pitched voice, her face pale.

Aisha tried to stay calm. She kept her head steady and walked up toward the mirage with strong eye contact. She blew out a deep breath. Her mouth forming an "O," she tried to touch it. Nothing happened. When the mirage pulled her toward the stone, she walked forward without hesitation.

An unseen force plucked her from the ground, lifting her higher and higher into the emerald mist. She soared above her town. There was her house, a mere speck below! She saw Kelimutu Volcano, and there she saw a brown mirage with a fiery face and jaws and long hands with claws for fingers trying to attack her. *Was that the dark power?* Her heart pounded in her chest.

Then all of a sudden, with a sickening lurch, she plummeted back on the ground, landing with a jarring thud! The green mirage thrust the stone into her hand and disappeared. Aisha was dizzy for a few moments, her thoughts whirled like a tornado, her vision blurring as she struggled to collect herself. She looked at the stone, searching for answers. It was a huge, shiny emerald, warm and gleaming. Leftover green vapor fumes emanated out of it.

"Who are you?" Aisha asked loudly, hoping the woman would reappear. There was no answer. Aisha looked around to find her sister.

To her shock, she saw Liya crouched next to a tree with her hands covering her eyes, shivering.

"Liya, there is nothing to be afraid of. I'm fine," said Aisha, consoling her sister.

"Who was that woman?" asked Liya. "It looked for a second like a green tornado was swallowing you. Are you okay?"

"I feel a bit dizzy from all the spinning," said Aisha.

"That was very scary, let's go back home," said Liya sternly.

Aisha put the emerald in her bag. "I don't want to go home just yet. Let's sit down for a while. This is a lot of excitement at the start of our journey."

Liya opened her knapsack and handed the container with *mie goreng* to Aisha. The sisters had a sumptuous lunch.

"If the woman is a magician, I wonder if this emerald is magical?" asked Aisha, thinking aloud.

They looked at each other and shrugged.

"We need to find out," said Aisha.

Aisha took the emerald out of the bag. She shook it and

rubbed it against her dress, but nothing happened. She walked back to the bubbling water and hot spring, slowly placing the emerald over the smoky sulfur water. The crystal levitated above the hot spring, its icy aura radiating outward and chilling the surrounding air. The hot spring's surface began to shimmer and gleam, and within moments, it had transformed into a solid sheet of ice.

Aisha squealed and walked in a fast strut toward Liya. She handed the emerald to her sister.

"You try it!" said Aisha.

Liya walked over to another hot spring. She placed the emerald close to another hot spring, but nothing happened— the hot vapor was still rising. Aisha walked over and touched the emerald. The vapor ceased. The hot spring died down immediately, freezing the water underneath.

"Perhaps this emerald has the power to cool down anything that is extremely hot, and only I can work its power," mused Aisha. "I wonder if it will work the other way. Do you think I can make fire?"

"Only one way to find out!" Liya held up the two sticks. Aisha scraped the crystal across the sticks, the emerald glowed with an inner fire as she rubbed it against the sticks. With a sudden flash, it ignited the sticks into a crackling flame.

"You made fire! You made fire!" Liya exclaimed, jumping up and down.

"That woman *must* have been a magician. Does this mean I have elemental magic?" Aisha asked with a wide grin, her eyes sparkling.

"What is elemental magic, Sis?" asked Liya.

"I read in a book at Grandma's that those who possess elemental magic can control one or more of the four elements of nature—fire, water, air, or earth."

"That is *so cool*, Aisha."

With a shout of glee, Aisha yelled and twirled Liya in the air. Gently putting Liya down, she bounced on tiptoe in excitement.

"Liya, I had a dream last night. The woman we saw looked very similar to the one who came to me in my dream. She was luring me to Kelimutu," said Aisha, finally able to recall where she'd seen the woman.

If the woman was indeed a magician, did that truly mean she had elemental magic? Could she control elements like fire and water? Had Aisha truly discovered her powers? What did that mean, and how was it connected to the dream?

CRYSTALIZED ROCKS

AISHA WAS REALLY EXCITED AND wanted to turn back home to tell her mother everything that had happened. But a voice inside told her to go on. The girls got up to continue their journey. They made their way toward Tiwu Ata Polo, which was connected to Tiwu Nua Muri Kooh Tai. Aisha had heard Liya talk about the "sister lakes" many times, so she was happy to finally get to see them with her.

As they approached the lake, Aisha glanced down in awe. "The water is so crystal clear and white." It was not red like her grandma had mentioned.

Liya looked down at the water. On the surface there was a fish floating lifelessly. "Aisha, look at that. Look at that fish. It's not swimming. Is it dead?"

"Can you help the fish with your magical healing powers?" asked Aisha.

Liya put her hand on the fish. Something gleamed; the lake instantly turned red, and all the stones and rocks in the water

transformed into red crystals.

Aisha rubbed her eyes in disbelief. "Impossible!" said Aisha as she reached out to touch the crystals. As she took a few crystals in her hand, her shoulders dropped and her sense of skepticism turned into awe. The sight was spectacular with the bright red stones reflecting the sun.

Liya cupped her hands together and picked up the dead fish. As she lifted the fish, it shivered and jumped back into the water.

"The fish is alive!" Aisha cried. "You brought it back to life, Liya." She watched the fish swim away, amazed at Liya's powers. All along she had been jealous of Liya, and suddenly she felt ashamed of herself. She walked up to Liya and put her arm around her shoulder.

Aisha and Liya hugged each other. As they were still tight in one another's arms, a green vapor arose, and the fish that Liya had just brought back to life splashed and swam toward her. Aisha watched as Liya gently held out her hand; the fish swam forward and something heavy landed in her palm. As the fish swam away, something appeared in Liya's hand: a big, shiny red stone—a ruby. Just as she lifted the ruby, Aisha observed a green vapor emerging from the lake.

Was this a reward for an act of kindness?

"This has been the best day of our lives," Liya said excitedly, jumping up and down. "Let me pick some of these red rubies

from the water. I'm sure Mama will be happy to see them."
She dropped a handful into her bag.

They looked at each other and smiled.

"We can trade them and buy Mama the beautiful shawl she wanted," Liya said.

"We need to go to the mysterious caves next."

"Can we visit the caves another time?" Liya asked. "I want to go back home and show the rubies to Mama now. Also, I don't think I want to hike anymore."

"Oh. Sure. I can't wait to show her what we discovered too," said Aisha.

They opened their knapsack, ate the last of their snacks, and started their journey back home. When Aisha turned back to the lake where Liya had found the ruby, a green wisp of vapor gently floated up into the cloud. Had she and her sister discovered two of the four mysterious stones needed to suppress the dark power in the dream?

If so, there were two more gems she had to find.

CALM AND PEACE

THAT NIGHT, AISHA AND LIYA sat down with their family in a semicircle around the fireplace. They had so much to share. Grandma brought them hot soup and fresh bread.

Aisha started. "For Liya and me, today was one of the best days of our lives. I have finally discovered my true destiny."

"Tell us more," said her mother. "What did you discover? Tell us everything!"

Aisha related all the events about the lakes, how she found the emerald, how a magician emerged from the green mirage, how she called out to her, and how she felt very different now. She noted the different feelings she encountered when touching the emerald and the sense of courage and strength she now felt.

"Ma, are you thinking what I'm thinking?" Zaha said, looking at Grandma.

Grandma nodded.

"All these years, I have been telling you that the Bajau woman who gave me the amethyst was a magician," said Zaha.

Grandma bent her head and shook it from side to side. "My inhibitions about the Bajau did not allow me to believe that there was a magician among them. You were right, Zaha!"

Aisha was happy that Grandma now believed Mama.

"From what Aisha has described, it appears that the magician who gave you the amethyst has appeared before Aisha in spirit and handed the emerald to her on her tenth birthday," said Grandma. "All this for my one act of kindness. I recall how upset the magician's young son had been when she gave Zaha the amethyst that day. He cried that it rightfully belonged to him, that the magic was his." Grandma shook her head.

"I wonder where the magician's little boy is now. He must be a grown man by now," said Zaha. She got up to hug Grandma. Grandma's reservations about the Bajau were finally erased now.

"Mother, now that you agree with me, can you tell me why the Bajau woman handed the amethyst to me?"

"She mentioned that when she saw you, she found you suitable to impart her healing magic. She said that you should always wear the amethyst for protection. She also said that if you had daughters, they too would have special skills. However, they would have to discover their unique powers for themselves.

"I didn't believe any of this," said Grandma, "because of my prejudice. That is why I did not mention this to you. But it looks like all her predictions are coming true."

"This is wonderful, Ma," said Zaha.

"We still have more to share," said Aisha, trying to get their attention. "Liya can tell you the rest."

"Mama," said Liya, excitedly showing all the rubies she had found. "The water in the lake turned red when I touched it, and all the rocks became red rubies. I even brought a dead fish back to life. When I put my hand in the water, the fish planted this ruby in my hand as a way of thanking me."

"It was in return for Liya's act of kindness!" Aisha beamed at Liya, who proudly showed the ruby to her family with a smile gleaming from one side of her face to the other.

"We have to be very thankful for the powers our little girls have discovered," said Grandma.

The family quietly ate their supper, pondering all the excitement. Afterward, Aisha and Liya cozied up with a blanket. The only sound was the whisper of the leaves rustling in the night. What the family was experiencing was pure happiness. Aisha watched as Mother and Grandma looked quietly at the stars.

11
HEALING TOUCH

THE NEXT DAY, AISHA WOKE up. Since Aisha had conquered her fear, her mother had given her and Liya permission to explore the caves on the very top of Kelimutu by themselves. They had heard various stories about the caves. Her mother had also explored these caves when she was young. The weather was perfect. Not too hot, but enough sunshine to keep them warm as they climbed.

Aisha got dressed. She walked up to the mirror and looked at herself. She felt more confident now. She reached out to the drawers next to the mirror and removed the big gleaming emerald the strange woman had given her. She walked over to her mother's chest of drawers.

"Ah! I found the right one," said Aisha as she removed a necklace with a missing pendant stone. She stuck the emerald into the pendant. It fit perfectly. She proudly fastened it around her neck and walked toward her mother.

"This is so beautiful," said her mother as she touched the

pendant. "Liya can do the same. I'm certain I have another pendant lying in the drawers in which Liya can put her ruby."

Liya walked up to the drawers to look through the jewelry and found a smaller necklace that was perfect for her neck. As Liya fastened the ruby necklace, the red light from the stone made her cheeks glow with a red hue.

She then pulled out a map her mother had made for them on a *lontar*—a palm-leaf manuscript. She packed it in their knapsack with some snacks and lunch.

"The caves are a lot of fun if you keep safe and avoid the dark tunnels," she advised. "It is best to go now when there is so much sunshine, but make sure you start descending the mountains before the sun sets."

The girls giggled, looking at each other, and promised to be safe.

When they got off the bus, they started their walk to the mountains on the path that was color-coded brown on the map, walking toward the tallest *ampupu*, or eucalyptus tree. Then they took a slight right at a grassy patch, heading across the rice paddy fields and up the mountains, making sure they stayed on the path.

The view got better and better as they ascended. As they climbed higher and higher, they no longer saw grass but red and black cedar trees. These trees had burned during the last Kelimutu eruption, the day she was born, and ten years later the scene still looked gloomy and hopeless. Aisha felt very sad and guilty looking at the barren trees. This was all her fault.

Before Aisha had realized it, Liya was already off the path, walking toward the burnt grove. She went to what was once a magnificent cedar, now a blackened trunk and sustaining only three branches. She laid her hand on a branch, feeling deep sympathy for the tree. She closed her eyes, imagining how it must have looked before the eruption. As Liya touched the branch, Aisha watched in wonder as she breathed new life into the tree.

Liya's ruby was shining. Aisha could not believe her eyes, and for a moment she thought that it was the glare from the sun making her see something different. She crossed over to where Liya stood and wiped her eyes, and in fact the whole tree was turning brown. Soon green leaves began to emerge from the cedar tree—the entire tree was alive again!

"Liya, open your eyes!" Aisha shouted. "Look what is happening to the tree!"

Liya opened her eyes and was stunned.

"This is what I imagined the tree would have looked like," she said. "Are you saying my imagination made the tree come alive?"

Aisha nodded. "I think it's your healing magic. I saw it as it was happening. Can you try again with this other tree? This one must have been really old and even more majestic."

Liya ran to the tree and closed her eyes. The ruby in her necklace shone again, and as she touched the branch, just the same as before, the entire tree came to life. Liya opened her eyes and looked down at her necklace; the ruby was shining brightly. The cedar tree had a healthy red hue, and its once-burnt branches were now covered with lots of green leaves.

Aisha jumped up and down jubilantly. "My sweet little sister, do you realize your healing powers are growing stronger? First the fish, now the trees. You have given life back to these trees. We have to get back home and tell Mama. She will be very happy." Even though Grandma and Mama knew about Liya's healing magic, healing at this scale was something really exciting.

They started descending the mountains excitedly, no longer in the mood to explore the caves. They had to tell everyone about the healing miracle. They boarded the next bus back to town.

As they arrived back in Moni, Aisha's Bajau friend Shelta saw them and came running over to see what the excitement was all about. "I have magic," said Liya, and the sisters explained what happened to Shelta. Shelta was so excited to learn about the magic she ran back to her family to tell them, and Aisha and Liya ran home.

When they got to the house, their mother was sitting down with Grandma. Aisha and Liya shared their stories,

and Mother was very excited to learn how Liya had used her inherited magical healing powers. Grandma got up to close the door.

"Look, there is a crowd gathered around the little Bajau girl . . . What was her name?" asked Grandma.

"Shelta, Grandma," said Aisha.

She turned back and asked the girls if they had told anyone. The girls nodded.

"We told Shelta everything," said Aisha. "All about Liya healing the trees and how her ruby shone as she healed them."

"There is a high possibility that she is sharing your story with everyone. I told you to stay away from them," said Grandma.

Aisha could see a crowd through the window. However, one person walked away from the commotion, glancing away from the tents. Aisha slowly made out the shadow of a hunchbacked man with a stick.

BAJAU LIFE

THE TREK TO KELIMUTU HAD made Aisha hungry for adventure.

"Liya, what should we do today?" asked Aisha, hoping Liya would have some ideas.

"Shelta promised to show us some swimming and diving tricks. Maybe we could do that today," said Liya.

"That sounds like fun," said her mother. "Bajaus are masters of the sea. Their children learn to swim before they walk."

The sisters had a light breakfast, changed into swim clothes, and walked to the Bajau tents. As they neared, they saw Bajau children splashing in the lake water. The rocky shoreline was decked with colorful gravel, a mix of shades of gray and white. A lonely piece of driftwood floated close to the lake shore, and a small turtle was trying to climb on the knobby log.

Liya jumped as a spindly-legged skimmer crab skittered close to her leg. The Bajaus were getting ready to maneuver their boats to get their day's catch. Fishing boats and row boats dotted the water.

Aisha looked at the majestic waterfall next to the lake. The water flowed elegantly, bubbling over the rocks. Against the backdrop of the sky, the waterfall looked blue, like a sheet of soft blue satin flowing from the top.

"The waterfall looks even more spectacular today," said Aisha as she heard the roar of the water pattering against the rocks. Bajaus were speaking with raised voices, and the children were laughing as they were splashing in the lake. The smell of water-saturated air, rich earth, and flowers by the lake shore was very pleasant. Since the day she hiked Kelimutu, her perception of everything around her had changed.

Liya nodded but was distracted by the children swimming in the lake. "Look at them! That little Bajau boy is only a year old," said Liya, fascinated. "Look how well he is swimming!"

Shelta suddenly emerged from the lake water and splashed them. "Do you want to swim with me?"

"Yes, but only if you teach us a few tricks," said Aisha.

"Watch me!" said Shelta and gracefully dove back into the water. Aisha and Liya just stared at each other in wonder. After about five minutes had passed, they got worried.

"What happened? Why is she still underwater?" Aisha asked one of the Bajau men who was watching the baby boy swimming.

"Don't worry about Shelta," said the man, "she is an expert. She can stay underwater for about ten minutes."

"Look what I found!" said Shelta, emerging from the water with two oysters. "They make such beautiful pearls! I brought two of them, one for you, Aisha, and one for you, Liya."

Shelta then walked over to the nearest fishing boat docked there. She went through the bag of fishing supplies and pulled out an oyster knife. The sisters watched as Shelta inserted the knife into the opening of the oyster shell. She then cut down on the oyster to halfway open it. She pulled open the shell completely. Aisha and Liya moved closer to Shelta, peering over the oyster to see what they would find. "I'm feeling the inside of the oyster to see if there's a pearl," explained Shelta.

"Look! There is a white pearl there," said Liya excitedly pointing inside. Slowly Shelta pulled the pearl out; it was beautiful, flawless, and white. Liya opened her palm to claim the pearl. Shelta then opened the second oyster the same way to retrieve a pink pearl. She handed this to Aisha.

"That was really nice of you," said Aisha, putting both pearls in her bag. She put the bag on the shore, and the girls jumped into the water. Fishes tickled Aisha's toes as she swam. Shelta showed them all the strokes she knew, but however long they spent, they could not master diving like Shelta; she was a natural swimmer and diver.

"We Bajau people have been called sea nomads. Our ancestors have lived at sea for more than a thousand years. We sometimes build houseboats and just float along. This is the first time I have seen my people put up tents," said Shelta.

"Why did they put up tents this time?" asked Aisha.

Shelta shrugged. "I don't know, but I'm happy I have new friends," she said, hugging Aisha.

The trio swam toward the waterfall. In the beginning Aisha felt the mist on her skin, and soon the cool slide of water washed over her head. Liya was scared at first, then she too joined the fun. Seeing Liya's hair sticking to her scalp, everyone laughed. Air bubbles slid across Liya's face. Aisha's vision was blurred under the splash of the waterfall, and all she could hear was the beat of the water falling over her head and shoulders. After spending a good amount of time splashing and giggling, the girls swam back toward the lake.

"How deep can your people dive?" asked Aisha.

"I know my grandfather was able to dive up to two hundred feet."

"It is amazing how your family just uses simple handmade goggles and spears to catch fish," said Aisha, watching the Bajaus fish. Aisha and Liya learned a lot about sea Bajaus that day.

"My father told me that we are going to trade supplies and search for precious items for a while. That is why we came ashore," said Shelta.

Aisha wondered what that meant. It sounded a bit fishy,

but she didn't want to suspect Shelta or the Bajaus. After all, she and her sister had had a great time and really enjoyed Shelta's company.

13

MYSTERIOUS CAVES

A WEEK LATER, AISHA AND Liya had not forgotten about the mysterious caves they had been planning to visit. The girls got up early at sunrise, packed their knapsacks, and set out on their adventure.

The first part of their hike was very smooth. The sisters walked through the meandering path decked with plants on one side and rugged rocks on the other side. Several tree roots crisscrossed the trail. Branches hung low from the trees in the path as if luring them to climb on them. Aisha stepped on the fallen leaves, crunching them as she walked through the shrubs of berries and wildflowers. A giant spiderweb caught her eye. A lonely spider was waiting patiently for its prey. Spectacular circles of web were spun in perfection. Birds chirped, and squirrels scurried up the tree trunks.

The sisters ascended the mountain and soon reached the spot where there were burnt trees, but with Liya's touch, the entire forest now enjoyed new life. The tall cedars and pines stood proudly with fresh needles, and there was no trace of the fire. The girls took a break, running around the renewed forest before having a quick lunch.

They then followed their mother's map until they reached the opposite side of the forest. It looked like the place where the caves were located. As they moved closer, they saw the opening of a gigantic cave. There were ropes connected to the mouth of the cave, which led inside.

"We hold those ropes and follow them so we do not get lost," Liya reminded her sister, recalling their mother's instructions.

Aisha analyzed the rigid, contoured surfaces of the cave. The entrance was arched and rocky, and the cave looked very big and roomy. Bumpy stone walls with fingerlings of tree roots grew through the crevices of the rocks. There were several claw marks, perhaps made by bears or mountain lions. They held the rope and, with one last moment to gather their bravery, walked inside. Bats flew through the descended ceilings.

"Ouch!" cried Aisha as she slipped and fell.

Liya turned on her torch. "Look, Sis! The ground is moist and damp."

Aisha held the wall of the cave and slowly got up. She looked around to get a sense of the space. Hieroglyphs—cave paintings—were all across the wall. Aisha wondered who could have painted them in such dim light. They seemed to tell a story. There was an old man in the painting; he sat on a stone near a fire pit. Several people—men, women, and children— were gathered around as if listening intently to what he was saying. *Must have been a leader, perhaps,* thought Aisha.

"Look here, Aisha," said Liya, breaking her thoughts as she pointed to a set of steps that seemed to lead somewhere. "Let's follow the rope and see where this takes us." Aisha slowly descended the steps, wanting to be more cautious after her first fall.

When they reached the bottom, Aisha looked around and said excitedly, "These look like underground tunnels!"

They followed the passageways. It was getting darker, so they made sure they continued to hold on to the ropes. "Look," said Liya, "there are underground rooms. There is even a courtyard!"

"This is amazing. Look at the stone walls," said Aisha, looking at the courtyard, which was unnaturally bright. "How is this place getting so much light when we're under the ground?"

"I don't know, but it's so cold in here," said Liya, shivering.

The two sisters saw that the courtyard was surrounded by shining pillars, and when they looked at the ceiling, they saw icicles that glowed brightly, hanging down, and at the same time, stalagmites protruded from the ground to join them. The colored, gleaming icicles made the cave look magnificent.

Aisha jumped in excitement. "I know a thing or two about icicles. Grandma taught me that the ones hanging from the roof are called stalactites, and those from the ground going up are called stalagmites."

The scene was spectacular, and the girls wished their family was with them. The icicles were red, green, purple, and snow white. As the girls walked by, shivering, they saw their reflections in the icicles.

"Mama said there would be a big surprise at the end of the cave. I bet this is what she meant," said Liya.

"No wonder Grandma brought Mama here when she was a child, and Mama came so many times. This is all so beautiful!" said Aisha in awe.

As they looked around, they saw that there were no more ropes beyond that point. It looked like a dead end. Except ... off to the side, there was a small dark passage. They were not supposed to venture anywhere that had no ropes. Their mother had been very clear about this.

"Looking inside for a while won't hurt," said Aisha. She peeked inside, but as she put a foot inside the dark passage, her loud scream echoed against the cave walls, shocking Liya. Her scream startled bats that were inside, and they rushed out in a flurry, dropping some of their prey—poisonous scorpions and small snakes. The girls ran back to safety.

They decided this was a good sign for them to stop their

adventure and head back out of the caves along the rope path. Liya decided they needed to collect a few colorful icicles to show their mother.

"There's no point. They will melt by the time we get home," said Aisha.

Still, Liya broke off a few purple, green, red, and snow-white icicles and put them in her bag.

They slowly retraced their steps through the dark tunnel until they reached the mouth of the cave. They heaved a sigh of relief that they had found their way back safely and began to make their way back down the mountain. By the time they had descended the slopes, Liya's bag was heavy and wet.

"It must be the icicles melting and filling the bag with water," teased Aisha. "I told you there was no point in collecting them."

Liya stopped and sat on the ground to take a look in the bag. As she peered in, a look of surprise lit up her face.

14
THE THEFT

"WHAT IS IT? WHAT'S WRONG?" As Aisha ran to Liya, she looked in the bag and was stunned; it was full of tiny gems—purple, green, red, and white. The crystals must have been hidden in the icicles, giving them their color, and when they melted they had left behind fascinating gems.

"Wait a minute," said Liya, pointing at one really big gem. It was sparkling, shining brightly in the sun. It was flawless.

"This is a *diamond*," Aisha yelled excitedly. They rushed home to show their mother.

Zaha was just finishing up with her last patient of the day and sending him home with medicinal potions. As they arrived, they saw the old man with the hunchback walking out. Aisha and Liya both froze.

Aisha had nothing against the Bajaus—she loved Shelta—but something about this man gave her the creeps. Liya felt the same.

"What was he doing in our house?" hissed Liya. They

waited and watched him leave. The girls dashed inside.

"Mama, who was that man? Why did he come to our house?" asked Aisha.

"He just came for some potions," said Mother. "He has been struggling with chronic pain in his legs, so I prepared him some medicine."

The girls were relieved.

"Although it is my duty to treat every patient," said Mother, "I'm a bit concerned. Apparently, he used to be a legendary smuggler, so he made a living by stealing."

"What did he steal?"

"He mentioned that when he was younger, he used to steal precious stones and sell them for a fortune," said Mother. "He did that to support his family until, one day when he was carrying loot, he had a fight with a rival group of smugglers, and he was terribly injured."

"That probably explains his hunched back," said Aisha. "But you should not be treating thieves, Mama."

Mother smiled. "He is no longer a thief. As a healer, it is my duty to help people, and sometimes patients share their stories with me. The only reason I'm sharing this with you is because I want you to be careful when you go to the Bajau tents—even though I think he is now a better man. There may be bad smugglers still trying to sort out their enmity with him."

"I was always scared of him, and now I'm even more scared," said Liya.

"We will stay away from him," said Aisha, hugging Liya.

"Let's forget about this now," said Mother. "I didn't mean to scare you. I'm glad you girls came home before it was dark. Tell me all about your adventure. Did you find the surprise in the cave?"

Liya had a beaming smile on her face, and she handed her bag to Mother.

Mother opened the bag and gasped, "Where did you get these gems? They are so tiny! Purple, green, red, and white. Where are they from?"

The girls shared their adventure, telling her all about the caves, the mysterious icicles, and how Liya decided to bring back a few only to find that they melted and turned into gems when they opened their bag.

"Your grandma and I have gone there several times, but not once did we see colorful icicles. We only saw white icicles. Did you touch any icicles in the cave?" asked Mother.

"Yes, we might have," said Aisha. "The ground was really slippery, so we may have held on to the wall of the tunnel."

"Perhaps your touch gave them this color," said Mother, sounding excited. "What is this?" she asked, pulling out the big diamond.

"We also found that when the icicles melted," said Liya.

"Wow, I didn't know the cave had diamonds," said Mother. "This is really precious—more precious than the ruby and emerald, Liya." Mother held it in her hand. "I will take it for safekeeping."

Could this be the third mysterious gem? thought Aisha.

As Mother was getting up to put the diamond away in a safe place, Liya's face turned white, and she pointed to her mother's neck. Mother looked down and realized her amethyst necklace was gone.

Liya ran to Grandma's house to tell her that the necklace was missing.

"I was afraid this would happen," Grandma said. "It was the Bajaus. I never trusted them." She came straight over to console Zaha because she knew how much the necklace meant to her.

Zaha was very upset. All of a sudden, she looked very weak and tired. She sank back in the rocking chair, disheartened, totally lost in thought. She rocked back and forth.

Aisha broke the silence. "I'm sure the hunchbacked man took the necklace when you were treating him! He told you he was a smuggler. Maybe he is still a thief."

Zaha shook her head. "Let's not start suspecting people. It could have been my fault. I may have simply lost it."

"Fine," Liya said. "Let's search the whole house." She dashed around the house, looking in every nook and corner.

After frantically looking both inside and outside the house and tracing all the places their mother might have gone that day, the girls realized they had to come up with a better plan.

"I knew the day the Bajaus settled down in our village no good would come of it," Grandma muttered. She then glanced at the precious stones spilling out of the bag. "Where did you get these?"

Aisha narrated the adventure of the mysterious caves and how they had taken the icicles only to realize they contained these precious stones.

"We should keep these safe. I will guard them. The Bajaus will come here to find the gems, and they will not think that anyone would entrust an old woman with gems, so they will be safer with me," Grandma said, then she picked up the bag and walked out of the house.

Aisha and Liya followed her, taking the diamond with them. Their mother was too anxious to worry about keeping the diamond safe.

Grandma entered her house. In the bedroom, she had an old, ripped painting of a volcano. Aisha had always wondered why she had it, for it seemed so out of place. She watched as her grandmother removed the painting from the wall, then carefully removed the painting from the frame, which was made of thin wooden pipes.

Grandma slowly poured the gems and diamond into the pipes and then fixed the frame back to where it was. She put the painting back into the frame and hung it on the wall.

"This is our little secret. Don't tell anyone, and definitely not your new friend Shelta," Grandma told Aisha and Liya.

NEW EVIDENCE

THAT NIGHT, AISHA HAD ANOTHER dream.

"You need to find the amethyst, Aisha. The mystery must be solved," said the woman in the green robe. "The amethyst is the fourth stone. Time is running out, Aisha. Suppress the dark power and unite the gems," said the woman, pulling Aisha toward a gigantic, ten-foot eagle statue. The mighty statue was covered in 24-karat gold and glittered in the bright sun.

Aisha followed the woman, frantically trying to hold on to the diamond, ruby, and emerald. As she stepped in her direction, a strong gust of wind pulled her with force; unable to keep her fingers clasped, she dropped the gems one after another, and by the time she reached the statue, it was too late.

The lava exploded from Kelimutu.

Aisha woke up in shock. What a terrible dream. She must find the amethyst. There was no time to lose. It was no longer just a mystery about her mother's missing necklace. It was the mystery of finding the last stone to suppress the dark power.

Aisha got up, determined to solve the mystery. The sisters spent the whole morning talking about the missing amethyst. Although the hunchbacked man was the obvious suspect, it would be utterly foolish of him to steal the amethyst because it was well-known that Mother wore it, and thus he would be easily caught trying to sell it in the village.

"I think we need to make a list of all the patients who came to our house yesterday," said Aisha.

Liya ran to open her mother's appointment book and examined the names of all of her patients for that day.

Liya read through the list. "First patient of the day was Mawar."

"Mawar is such a good, old friend of Grandma," Aisha said, "and she has been so nice. I love listening to her stories."

"She must have come to talk to Mama about her back pain," Liya said. "It has been so long since we heard stories from her."

"We should ask later if she remembers seeing Mama with the necklace when she treated her."

"Great idea!"

"We should do that with all the patients on the list," said Aisha.

Liya looked back down at the list. "Permata. Isn't she the Bajau woman who wears lots of jewelry?"

Aisha looked at her. "Yes, she would weigh a ton less if she took off all her jewelry. She wears heavy earrings studded with crystals. She also wears many bangles around her neck, on her arms, and even her legs. And she has several waistbands to keep herself looking slim."

"Her neck almost looks like a giraffe's," said Liya, forcing Aisha to giggle.

"I wonder how Mama treats her with all the jewelry on?" said Aisha. Suddenly, a thought occurred to her. She ran to Zaha. "Mama, when you treat Permata, do you ask her to take off her jewelry?" she asked.

"Yes, I have to," said Zaha. "Most of the pain she gets is from the tight waistbands she wears and those heavy bangles around her neck. It takes me almost an hour with her because she needs time to take the jewelry off. Yesterday I lent her a bag because I wanted her to take a break from wearing them while she was receiving treatment."

"I would love to see how she looks when she takes them off."

Suddenly, another thought occurred to Aisha: what if Mother's necklace had fallen when she was treating Permata, and Permata accidentally took it as she was scooping all her jewelry into her bag? They should definitely check with Permata. They wrote down their suspicion.

Liya looked back at Mother's logbook. The next person on the list was Intan, Shelta's father. "Why did Shelta's father come to see you?"

Mother looked up. "He had many bad bruises. He told me he had fallen as he was climbing his tent to fix a patch," she said. "It looked more like he had been injured in a fight because you don't usually get so many bruises all over the body from a fall like that. But as a healer, I don't ask too many questions. If they don't want to tell me the truth, they don't. Also, I gave him medicine to take to his wife. Interestingly, Grandma says she thought he seemed very familiar. She mentioned she had seen someone with a moon-shaped scar on his cheek like his before."

Aisha wrote down the observation. The sisters would need to somehow check with Shelta about her father.

DESPERATE PATIENT

"ZAHA, HELP ME!" YELLED SOMEONE at the door. Aisha rubbed her eyes. She looked at the clock near the candlelight. It was past midnight. The banging on the door got louder. "Zaha, are you home?" It sounded like a desperate old man's voice.

Zaha quickly woke up. She peeked through her window to check who was knocking at the door this late. "Yoshi, it's you," said Zaha, running toward the door and opening it wide for him to enter.

Yoshi was an old man with a wrinkled face and hands. He was clad in beige *kurta* and white *dhoti*. He had a handkerchief wrapped on his right hand that was soaked in blood. Aisha got up to get him a chair to sit down.

Zaha got immediately to work. She unwrapped the cloth around his hand. It revealed a severe, deep cut that was bleeding profusely. Aisha ran to get her mother the kit she always used for stitching deep cuts. While Zaha was treating Yoshi, Aisha ran to the kitchen to fetch a glass of water for the patient. He was looking like he would faint any minute.

After her mother was done, she made him lie down on the patient bed. A lot of thoughts came into Aisha's head. *Who was this man? How was he so severely injured?* She hoped her mother would ask him. Zaha instead was just putting a blanket over him and checking his pulse. Soon she watched as Yoshi fell asleep.

It was pretty late in the night, and Liya was still asleep despite all the commotion. Aisha walked to Liya's bed and snuggled in with her sister and fell asleep.

THE SCULPTOR

THE NEXT MORNING AISHA WOKE up to mumbled whispers. She saw her mother talking to Yoshi as he was sipping hot tea. His right hand was bandaged, and he was holding the teacup with his left hand. He looked much better. His face was no longer flushed.

"Thank you, little apprentice," said Yoshi, looking toward her.

"Aisha is learning the tricks of my trade really fast."

Aisha was embarrassed with so many compliments. "How is your hand?" she asked Yoshi in an effort to divert the attention she was getting.

"Your mother is a magician! Goodness, I feel much better. Now I can get back to work."

"No, you will not," said Zaha sternly looking at him. "You need to give your hand some rest. No sculpting for another ten days at least."

"Are you a sculptor?" asked Aisha, looking at Yoshi. He

pulled out a small bag and handed it over to Aisha. She untied the knot at the top of the bag and peeked inside. There were so many small idols made of black stone chiseled to perfection.

"These are my miniature samples of all the statues I have sculpted. The stone idols I sculpt are typically around ten to twenty feet in height."

Aisha placed them on the table one by one. "Shiva," she said, looking at the idol that had a meditative man with a snake wound on his neck; he was in a seated posture with his eyes closed. "Hanuman," said Aisha, looking at the next idol of a majestic monkey king holding a mountain on his hand.

"It is Hanuman, the monkey warrior who helped King Rama conquer the wicked ten-headed demon Ravana," said Yoshi.

"I have just started reading the Book of Ramayana and I love Hanuman, he is such a brave and loyal warrior."

"Would you like to see the mighty bird, Golden Garuda, that I'm sculpting?" asked Yoshi.

"Yes," said Aisha, and another voice echoed behind her. Liya was wide awake and already examining the small versions of the idols.

"I can take you to the Kelimutu mountain tomorrow and show you the idols. I will be installing the Garuda in a few days at the top of the mountain," said Yoshi. "I don't normally make golden statues, but this one is very special. I also need to decorate this idol; you two girls can give me some ideas."

Aisha was excited and saw Liya's face light up. "Can we go today?" Aisha asked.

He turned toward Zaha for consent. "I want to join you," said Zaha, "but today I have a big list of patients. And I'm worried they will come back to get you, Yoshi. You should stay in the village a little longer."

"Who is trying to harm Yoshi?" asked Liya in a concerned voice.

"The statues he is sculpting are very precious, especially the Golden Garuda," said Zaha. "The Indonesian Prime Minister himself has commissioned Yoshi to build this statue. The smugglers are after the statue, and it may not be safe for Yoshi to go up the mountain," said Zaha.

"They cannot find the Garuda. I have it safely hidden in the mysterious caves. Those smugglers think they can find out the secret spot by threatening me, and when they realized I would not utter a word about the statue, they attacked me," said Yoshi.

"Garuda, the mighty bird, protected me when he swooped from the sky and scared them away."

"Garuda is real?" asked Liya.

"Garuda can be seen only by those who believe in him," Yoshi said with firm faith. Aisha's chest swelled in pride. She had not only seen Garuda, but he had also put a hand on her head, blessing her to be brave. Perhaps she had found her destiny. She will save Moni at any cost, and only she can do this.

KEY SUSPECTS

AFTER YOSHI LEFT, AISHA OPENED her mother's patient diary to see the list of patients that visited their home the day the amethyst went missing. Considering the sisters were not climbing Kelimutu today, they had enough time to interrogate each of the patients.

First, they headed to Mawar's house, carrying some fresh bread and fruit. It was customary to take some gifts when visiting an older relative. Although Mawar was not technically related to them, she was like a grandmother to them. And really they were hoping the gift would convince her to tell them one of her stories.

Mawar opened the door and welcomed the girls with a warm hug. She was so excited she immediately sat Aisha on her lap. She brushed the hair back from Aisha's face and looked at her intently. "You look just like your mother. Your eyes, so beautiful."

She tried to lift Liya too, but her back wouldn't allow it.

Liya smiled and jumped up onto her lap. She looked at Liya and gave her a big kiss on her cheek. "I can't believe how fast you have grown. You look so much like your sister did at your age." She looked at Liya's hand. "Do you know you have magic?" She winked at Liya.

Liya excitedly related to Mawar how the whole forest had come alive with her touch. They spent a few hours talking as Mawar served them nice hot porridge and bread. Aisha then realized it was almost noon, and they had to visit the other "suspects."

Quickly, Aisha asked Mawar if she had seen the necklace on her mother during her treatment.

"Yes," Mawar said, "that is Zaha's identity. I would have surely noticed if it was missing. I remember seeing it."

The girls thanked Mawar for the information and the meal. They set out toward the Bajau row of tents, where music filled the air. Intan, Shelta's father, sat playing the fiddle. His shirt was folded up in one hand with a bandage. He also had a bandage on his leg. The dressing looked like the kind their mother normally used for her patients.

Shelta saw them and came out running. "Come!" she exclaimed and pulled them into her tent. Shelta was wearing an orange skirt and a yellow blouse. Her blouse had a blue patch on it. It looked like it had been torn and then stitched back together. This was the first time they had been inside Shelta's home.

It was very small, and the tent had several patches on the roof.

Aisha looked up at the roof and asked, "Did you have a recent tear on your tent?"

Shelta shook her head. "No, those were there when we first put the tent up. It looks flimsy, but it is really tough."

Liya looked at Aisha. Intan had not fallen fixing their tent then. It must have been from something else.

Shelta showed them an old trunk sitting in the corner. She opened it and pulled out several ragged dolls. One of the dolls, although dusty, was beautiful; its eyes looked almost real. The doll had a long pink dress with a blue border and frills at the bottom. It carried a fan.

"My mother looks like this doll," Shelta said.

"Where is your mother?" Liya asked curiously.

Shelta pointed to the curtain in their tent. "Shhh! She's asleep. Today is the first time I have seen Mother feeling better. We spent some time talking, and she was able to walk around without any pain," said Shelta. "My father says she will get better soon. My mother is a very talented woman. She used to weave beautiful baskets and blankets, and Father would take them and sell them for money. We had food, clothes to wear. I was very happy. Until one day she felt sick. We have been moving from place to place in search of a cure for her."

The girls felt really sad listening to Shelta's story. They

hoped Shelta's mother would recover and get back on her feet. They consoled Shelta and then asked her to show them the tent of the old hunchbacked man.

"Why do you want to go to Banyu's tent?"

"Nothing important. Our mother asked us to check on him, for she had given him some health potions," fibbed Aisha.

Shelta walked outside, pointed to a very tattered tent, and then went back to join her family.

They walked up to the tent of the hunchbacked man and peeked inside. They could see him walking to light a candle. He had a few blankets piled up, and there were several bags piled in a corner. The girls wondered if he was getting ready to sleep. Instead, he walked outside. The girls thought fast and immediately hid behind a bush next to the tent. They were so afraid, they tried to hold their breath. They did not want to get caught sneaking.

He slowly left the tent with his stick and walked about fifty yards. They quickly crept inside. There were piles of bags—very bulky sacks tied with strings. The tent smelled very strange, and there was leftover bread on the floor and the smell of old food.

"Yikes! Looks like he never cleans up after eating," said Aisha.

"He definitely needs to tidy up his tent. Mama would never let us be this messy."

They looked around under the blankets near the pots and pans. They did not find the amethyst necklace. Quickly, they darted out of the tent.

Just when they thought they were free, strong hands grasped them by the scruffs of their necks.

19
STRANGE ENCOUNTER

AISHA AND LIYA FROZE. A woman in a long, flowing red dress with a veil on her head held Aisha. Over her dress she wore an orange, full-sleeved blouse. Angry eyes peered through the translucent golden veil. "What do you think you are doing snooping around in our tents?" she screamed angrily. "Are you trying to steal something?"

Aisha swallowed hard and tried to get out a word. "N-no, we didn't steal anything! We came to meet our friend, Shelta, and we wandered away afterward."

The woman sneered as if she didn't believe them. Her grasp on Aisha was still very tight, and it hurt. She had let Liya go, as Liya was not carrying a bag.

"We are very sorry," Liya said quickly. "We did not mean any harm. Can you please let go of my sister?"

The woman let go, her bangles jingling. "Just keep away from my tent!"

She walked away, and as she did, they noticed something

very familiar about her. They looked closer.

"She has a very long neck," said Liya. The girls looked at each other.

"Was that Permata?" both exclaimed at the same time.

Just as they were deciding where to go and what to do next, they saw Shelta running toward them looking very excited. "Something wonderful happened today! Will you come to my house?"

The girls did not want to disappoint Shelta, and this might also be a great way to meet Shelta's father and get more clues from him. They followed Shelta back to her home. The white curtain that had been closed the last time was now open. They heard a faint voice, and Shelta's father walked out of the tent to invite the girls inside. He looked jubilant.

"The Lord has listened to our prayers," he said.

"My mother is out of her bed after a year! She is better!" exclaimed Shelta.

As the girls walked through the small portion of the tent that was once closed behind a curtain, they saw a beautiful, frail woman sitting up in the chair with a big smile. She looked exactly like the doll Shelta had shown them. She held a bowl full of what looked like hot soup, taking small sips.

"Are you the friends that Shelta tells me about?" she asked. "I am so glad that you keep her company. You know, Shelta is very reserved. I was her only friend, and after I fell ill, she was very somber until she met you both. Thanks for being such great friends!"

Aisha was very happy for Shelta. Shelta's father, Intan, asked the girls to stay for supper. They immediately accepted the invitation. This would be a great way for them to learn more about Shelta and her family. Intan was cooking a special dinner of fish and sea cucumber.

While he was getting this ready, Shelta showed them her collection of pearls. She often dove down to search for oysters and had gathered many rare natural pearls that were perfect round spheres, white and light pink in color. Shelta also showed them baroque pearls, which were irregular and asymmetrical, and they came in different shapes such as a rice grain, a corn kernel, or a pear. Soon they got the call from Intan that supper was ready.

Shelta ran to help her father. They laid out a small low table outside the tent. She brought out three mats for them to sit on.

"We can help set up for dinner," said Aisha, offering to carry the food and the bowls.

Aisha and her sister carried the sea cucumbers and cooked fish and set them on the table.

With dinner ready, Shelta brought a small tray table for her mother with food. She then opened the front cover of the tent so she could stay in her chair but also see them and hear their conversations.

Shelta related many diving escapades. They talked about how they enjoyed going from one place to another, and they also talked about how they had once built and lived in stilt houses. The sisters learned quite a lot about the Bajau life that night.

Soon it was time to leave. They thanked their hosts for their hospitality and slowly walked back home.

What a day it had been, so exciting from hunting down suspects, to a close encounter, to having dinner with Shelta and her family. Although they hadn't solved the mystery yet, they felt they were getting closer.

UNEXPECTED INVITATION

THE NEXT MORNING, AISHA HEARD a knock on the door. On opening the door, to her pleasant surprise, she saw Yoshi, the master sculptor with his sack of miniature idols.

"Good morning," said Yoshi. "Is your mother at home?"

"Ma, Yoshi is here to meet you," said Aisha. Her mother came out of the kitchen.

"How is your hand?" asked Zaha, walking toward Yoshi to examine his hand. She asked him to sit down and slowly untied the bandage. Aisha saw that the bruise was much better. She watched as her mother slowly moved the arm. Yoshi seemed to have regained his range of motion as well.

"I hope you and the girls can come and see my statues today," said Yoshi, looking at Zaha.

"Yes," said Aisha before her mother could even utter a word. "Ma, please let us see the Golden Garuda and the other statues today. Please, Ma, let us go."

"I'm relatively free today. I have only two patients who need to collect their herbal potions," said Zaha. "Aisha, if you can run along to Grandma's house and ask her to cover for me at the clinic for a few hours, she can hand over the medicines to the patients."

"Yes, Ma." After informing Grandma about their day's plans, Aisha came back home. Seeing Liya still in bed, Aisha walked toward her sister.

"Liya, wake up! Yoshi is taking us to see the Golden Garuda," said Aisha excitedly. Liya could barely open her eyes. Aisha tugged at her blanket and repeated, "Liya, wake up. Don't you want to see the Golden Garuda?" asked Aisha.

"Why do we have to go this early?" said Liya, still sleepy.

"My statues are inside the Liang Bua cave close to the town of Ruteng. It is about a four hour bus ride," said Yoshi.

In about twenty minutes, the girls were ready and sat at the table as their mother served rice flour pancakes with coconut and palm sugar syrup. Aisha's mother always made mouth-watering pancakes.

After breakfast, Zaha packed a knapsack quickly for the hike to the mountains. Yoshi led the way, and the three of them followed him to the Moni bus station.

GOLDEN GARUDA

THEY BOARDED THE BUS TO Ruteng in the Manggarai district. The bus had very few passengers that day as it was off peak time. It was a two-seater bus. Aisha sat next to Yoshi, eager to hear more about the cave. Liya sat behind them next to Zaha.

"Liang Bua is a limestone cave slightly north of the town of Ruteng," said Yoshi.

"The cave is massive—about fifty meters deep, forty meters wide, and fifteen meters high."

"Is the cave going to be cold?" asked Aisha. Liang Bua translated to "cold cave" or "cool hole" in the local Manggarai language.

"Yes, I hope your mother brought some shawl wraps for you."

"I did. I have enough shawls to keep us warm," said Zaha.

"When I occupied the cave to start sculpting, I excavated several fossils of Komodo dragons and small Stegodons," said Yoshi. "I can show you some of the fossils, and if we have time,

I can also teach you how to use stone tools to excavate."

Aisha watched the sunbaked road through the window of the bus. The countryside was now even more open; there were no houses, just green pastures. Tall stalks of corn and rice filled the fields. It was the time to harvest. As the bus took them deep into the road, Aisha saw grazing cattle. Scruffy bushes and stunted trees dotted the land. Soon Aisha fell asleep.

A sudden jolt of the bus woke her. It had been nearly four hours. They had finally reached Liang Bua. They got down one by one from the bus. Yoshi led them to a large, open-mouthed cave. Aisha looked at the majestic cave with a cathedral ceiling. It was formed out of stalactites.

"Long ago this cave was formed with Miocene limestone and now is adorned with numerous small stalactites. The ground of the cave is covered with a thick layer of sediments. As you can see, the Miocene limestone is hard, slightly crystalline, compact, and creamy colored. It is massive in parts but some layers are richly fossiliferous," said Yoshi as they walked deeper into the cave. He seemed to know a lot about rocks.

Yoshi led them through the cave into a dark tunnel. He lit the pathway with a glass kerosene lantern. There was a huge rock at the dead end of the tunnel. Yoshi pointed the lantern to a small impression of an elephant at the top of the rock. He pulled out a small hook and dug this in to the center of the impression and pressed against it. Slowly the rock slid open.

They were now looking into a huge inner cave open to the sky. Two giant elephant statues stood on either side of the entrance, almost like they were guarding the cave. Sun shone on the marvelous statues. Each of them was huge, about twenty feet or more.

The first statue was of the Hindu deity Shiva in a meditative posture. He was seated cross-legged with two of his eyes opened. There was a third eye that was closed at the center of his forehead. He had a snake on his neck and was holding a long trident. This statue was about twenty-five feet tall. In front of the statue was Nandi, the giant bull that carries Lord Shiva. The Nandi carving was exquisite.

The next statue, the goddess Durga, showed the depiction of when she was victorious after vanquishing the buffalo demon Mahisha. The statue was sculpted to show eight hands for Durga, each carrying different weapons such as a conch, discus, lotus, sword, bow and arrow, trident, mace, thunderbolt, snake, and flame.

After this stood a mighty statue of the monkey king Hanuman.

Yoshi led them to the corner of the cave where there was a huge yellow cloth dangling from the ceiling. It was a twenty-foot tall and wide curtain. "Come here to see the most precious of all."

As he pulled the curtain, everyone gasped.

22
MAGNIFICENT STATUE

YOSHI STOOD FROZEN WITH HIS eyes bulging.

"This can't be true. This can't be . . ." he said, shaking his head in denial. Tears swelled up in his eyes and he moved away from them.

Aisha saw broken pieces of stone everywhere. It almost looked like the side of the cave had been forced open. She examined the stone walls; there was visible dirt and debris, as if there was a recent landslide. However, the broken stones were only at the very spot where Yoshi claimed the statue stood.

Yoshi sat in the corner, folding his arm against his stomach and sniffing and wiping at his nose. The muffled sound of the wind in the trees outside incremented the sudden feeling of cold and heaviness that Aisha felt. Her mother sat beside Yoshi, one hand on his shoulder.

Aisha hoped she could help Yoshi in some way. It must be hard for him to see the Golden Garuda missing. She had to find some clues, and she had to find them fast. Whoever took the statue could not have gone far.

"Aisha, look at these foot marks on the ground," said Liya, her voice cracking as she pointed to the several giant footsteps left behind. Wind shrieked through the hollows of the caves. Liya was shivering. As Aisha walked over toward her sister, her gaze fell on the stone walls. Her stomach clenched at the sight of red stains.

"Blood! Fresh blood!" A chill of fear ran through Aisha's spine. This was a masterminded theft, and the impressions left in the sand appeared fresh. The stones on the ground were wet, although there were no signs of a body of water around. Aisha touched the wet ground and scooped up the wet sand and stones. She smelled it.

"Yech, this is gross," said Aisha, instantly moving away from the foul smell.

"Probably sweat," Liya said, disgusted.

The commotion from Aisha forced Yoshi and Zaha to walk toward her.

"Fresh blood, indeed," said Zaha, examining the stain. "The criminals must have got cut against the sharp edges of the rocks here." Zaha glanced at the pointed edges protruding from the side wall of the cave. There were pieces of torn yellow cloth across the ground. "They must have dragged the heavy statue through here."

"The width of the trail does match up to the width of the

statue," confirmed Yoshi. "The statue weighs over four tons. You would need at least fifteen to twenty people to carry this out of the cave."

The trail stopped after over fifty feet. There were only footsteps after that, but no sign of dragging.

"It is almost as if the statue disappeared here," said Aisha.

23

THE GEM THIEF STRIKES AGAIN

AISHA, LIYA, AND ZAHA WENT home exhausted. Recalling the series of events in their minds, they went to bed and soon fell asleep, tired from all the running around that day.

The next morning they woke up when Grandma knocked on their door. Her eyebrows were furrowed, and she was sweating profusely.

"What happened, Grandma?" asked Aisha. "You look very upset."

Grandma walked inside, stomping in anger. "The thief has struck again!" she said, clenching her fists. "I will not let them get away with it!"

Somebody had broken into her house. Aisha ran with Liya behind her over the road to Grandma's house to see what had happened. She looked around and everything was strewn about—utensils, clothes, everything.

"Did you not hear any noise in the night?" asked Aisha when Grandma had caught up with them.

"When I got up early this morning, everything was okay. I went to the well to draw water. When I came back, I saw that someone had broken into the house. They have some nerve, stealing in the morning," said Grandma, biting her lips.

Liya nudged Aisha. "Let's check if the old painting is still there."

"No, it is gone," Grandma responded sadly. "The thieves were very clever. They knew I'd hidden the gems there."

Aisha hugged Grandma and tried to console her. "Grandma, please sit down and don't worry."

"We'll find the thief soon," said Liya.

"We found many clues yesterday," said Aisha. She nudged Grandma to sit down; the old woman was still very upset. The girls tried to tidy up and put everything back where they belonged.

"Look what I found!" said Liya as she lifted a torn piece of golden cloth. It was caught on the edge of some broken wood from the window.

"The thief or thieves must have broken through the window and jumped in when Grandma was at the well," said Aisha. "This fabric looks familiar. It is similar to the veil that mean woman was wearing two days ago."

Grandma's ears perked up, and she got up from the chair. "Tell me all about it. Which woman are you talking about?"

The girls told Grandma all about the events before they

visited the cave with Yoshi. She was still worried that the amethyst might have landed in the wrong hands.

"You girls have been very brave. I'm so proud of you," said Grandma. "Now we will tell your mother, and then you must let us—the adults—handle it from now on. We can go to the Bajau tents now and inquire."

"The thieves are very clever, and they may also be dangerous," said Aisha as she pointed to a bruise on her neck. "We need to outwit them with our powers and our clever thinking. Please give us one more chance, and we can find more clues about that woman!"

"Also, Mama is very busy with patients today. We do not want to lose any more time," said Liya.

Finally Grandma gave in. "I will come along and wear my cloak and sit under the big, tall tree close to the Bajau tents. If I don't hear from you or you don't meet me back at the tree before evening, then I will send out a search team for you both. Stay safe and good luck!"

The girls hugged Grandma and promised to be cautious.

OUTWITTING THE THIEF

Aɪsʜᴀ ᴀɴᴅ Lɪʏᴀ ʜᴇᴀᴅᴇᴅ sᴛʀᴀɪɢʜᴛ for Permata's tent. They could hear the jingling of her bangles and saw her shadow walk inside the tent. There was no point in going in now. They hid close to the bushes, hoping she would leave.

"Hopefully she'll go out. Then we can quickly sneak into her tent and find clues," said Aisha.

As if Permata had heard them, she hurriedly walked out of the tent clutching a bag close to her chest. She had a worried look on her face.

"Did you see that bag she had? We need to follow her."

"But what about searching her tent?" whispered Liya. "We have to see if any of Grandma's things are there."

"Let's split up. I will follow her."

"Okay. I'll check out the tent."

But when Permata dashed into Shelta's tent, Aisha couldn't follow her. She stayed outside the tent and tried to see what was happening. *Why is Permata going to Shelta's house?*

"Let us return everything. I don't want to get into any trouble," said Permata. "I wish I knew the amethyst was the healing gem. Look what I did!"

Aisha peered into the tent to see what Permata was holding. *Those are the gems Liya and I found. She must have broken into Grandma's house.*

Permata looked at Intan and said, "I stole again, and this time I stole a bag full of tiny gems and a big diamond."

"We will not need them," said Shelta's mother. "I know you both stole the gems out of your concern for me, so that their power could heal me. You did not mean any harm. You both meant well. I'm healed now, so now we must tell the truth and return everything to Zaha."

"Never! This rightfully belongs to me," said Intan, getting up and waving his hands in the air in agitation. He threw several objects out of the tent in anger. Something almost hit Aisha in the face. She ducked and picked up the object, a worn-out book that looked like a diary.

Aisha was shocked to hear all this. *Why was Intan claiming it belonged to him? Poor Shelta. How would she feel if she knew her father's truth?* Aisha tucked the book in her pocket.

Worried someone would see her, she hid in a group of bushes, thinking about what to do next.

Finally, Aisha decided she would find Liya, go home, and talk everything through with her mother. But as Aisha was trying to sneak away, someone grabbed her from behind, and before she knew it, a handkerchief was thrust over her nose and mouth.

When Aisha woke up, she had a throbbing headache. She was very dizzy and confused. She felt cold, and she was shivering. What had happened to her? All she could remember was that someone had put a strange-smelling handkerchief on her nose and knocked her out. She contemplated who this could have been when she saw the handkerchief lying next to her. There was fine stitching on the handkerchief. Looking closely, she saw it had the initial "B" and an embroidered water motif.

Could this be Banyu's handkerchief? She looked around. She was indeed in Banyu's tent, surrounded by bags full of things he had stolen.

He must be a big-time thief to have so much loot. I'm in big trouble now. Aisha wished she had not wandered off to investigate by herself. She tried to move her hands, but they were tied by ropes. She hoped that her mother would start to search for her soon. *I don't know how long they'll take. I'm trapped.* Just then, she heard some rumbling sounds and gruff voices.

"Why did you bring her here, you fool? We are going to be in a lot of trouble. Stealing loot I know, I have been doing that all my life. But kidnapping a child? No, we are in serious danger."

Aisha was struggling to figure out who that was. She slowly took a peek.

"I will not support this," said Banyu. "I'm no longer a criminal. My smuggling days are long gone. I want you to free this innocent child. You can defame me for all I care for the smuggling your gang is doing, but I want no harm to come to this girl."

"Where do you think we can run with all the loot?" a tall burly man with a beard asked. "We need your tent as a hideout. After we leave, the townspeople will kick you out, thinking you stole all this." The man laughed.

"Please leave this town. Go to the smugglers' cave on the other side of Kelimutu Volcano. Everyone is afraid Kelimutu may erupt, and soon they will evacuate the town. There you will be safe, and your loot as well."

"That is a clever idea from a foolish man. For once, you speak sense," said the wicked-looking man.

"I hope the poor girl is okay," said Banyu sadly. "You put too much chloroform on the handkerchief. She will be asleep for hours. I should not have listened to your threat and stolen the anesthesia from Zaha's house in the first place."

Aisha heard steps coming toward her, so she pretended to be unconscious and put her face back down. "The girl looks all right. She is still knocked out," said Banyu, stroking Aisha's hair with affection. She felt him loosening her ropes.

So, Banyu was a good man. Aisha felt ashamed for suspecting him. Aisha heard a lot of sounds, but she didn't budge. She assumed they were packing the loot up. There was a lot of rumbling, shoving, and grunting.

At last, things quieted down. When she heard nothing for a while, she felt it was safe to peek. All the voices were faint, and it seemed as if they had departed. She lifted her head slightly. The entire tent was empty. Every last bag of stolen goods was gone. Her heart sank.

Stealing from her townspeople meant that they would have nothing left to trade for food and necessary supplies for their homes and their children. Aisha had to do something, but she felt very dizzy and soon fell asleep.

25

RECOUNTING THE DAY'S EVENTS

AISHA WOKE UP SEVERAL HOURS later. The tent was empty. She had to escape. She looked at her hands and found that the ropes were loose; she vaguely recalled Banyu loosening the knots. She freed her hands and deliberately tried to get up. Her legs felt so heavy, so she just sank back down. There had to be a way to escape before they came back. As she looked around, she saw a pile of kindling stacked in the corner. She crawled slowly to the firewood, dragging her sluggish feet. She drew out two logs, and closed her eyes; she had to get her fire power working. But nothing happened. She focused and concentrated. At last, lifting her hands up in the air, she touched the two logs together, and a small spark erupted. Slowly the firewood ignited, and there was a small bonfire in the tent. She tugged at the top of the tent and pushed a pole right through it, causing a tear. She wanted someone to see the smoke coming from the tent; she had to get help. As thick smoke emanated from the tent, as if in response, she heard her mother's voice. Was she dreaming? Had she got help so fast? Sure enough, her mother and Liya walked into the tent.

THE ESCAPE

"We have been searching for you," said Liya, rushing to Aisha. Her mother walked toward Aisha. She picked up the handkerchief from the floor and sniffed it. She noted the letter "B" on the handkerchief. "This will give us a clue," said her mother as she tucked it in her coat pocket.

"Hurry, let us go, before the kidnappers return," said her mother. Aisha could barely stand up. She felt faint. Her mother helped her. Slowly, with Liya and Mother on either side, she walked out of the tent toward their home.

After they were about a kilometer away, her mother said, "Somebody stole the anesthesia bottle from my clinic yesterday. I'm the only one in this town who has any."

Liya pulled out the kerchief from her mother's coat.

"There is a letter 'B' marked on the handkerchief," noted Liya.

"This is Banyu's, but he did not kidnap me. The smugglers kidnapped me," said Aisha. "Banyu was threatened by the smuggler gang to steal the bottle of chloroform from you, Mama. The smugglers sedated me with a handkerchief dipped in the liquid, and they took me to Banyu's tent so that suspicion would fall on poor Banyu."

They were now close to home. Aisha's mother opened the door, and slowly Aisha sat down in the living room chair, her mother and Liya next to her.

Aisha slowly sat up straight and explained what had happened. She told them about Permata and Intan stealing the amethyst, diamond, and other gems and about Intan claiming that he was the rightful owner of the amethyst.

"This is a serious crime. Stealing, and now kidnapping my child. They cannot get away with this!" said Mother angrily. "I don't understand. Why did the smugglers knock you out? What were they afraid of?"

"They must have been afraid that I knew about their loot. I snuck into Banyu's tent because I suspected that he had stolen the amethyst," said Aisha. "Permata caught me snooping, but later when I was near Shelta's tent, the smugglers knocked me out and used Banyu so suspicion would fall on him. I feel bad for suspecting Banyu; he had good intentions."

"Where did they say they were going?" asked Mother.

"They mentioned a smugglers' cave on the other side of Kelimutu," said Aisha. "When I was gone, did you manage to retrieve the amethyst, Liya? Did you find it? Tell me everything."

Liya enthusiastically shared her story: "After we split up, I snuck into Permata's tent. Everything was so colorful inside. In the corner was a chest that gleamed with crystals. The top of the tent glittered with their reflections. At first, I stood there admiring all the glitter. Suddenly I heard a scratch. I froze. I was so scared.

"'Meow!' A black cat crawled out from behind the curtains. It peered at me," said Liya.

"I quickly opened the chest. There were many glittering crystals inside, along with many dozens of different types of bangles, necklaces, and anklets.

"Then I looked around the cooking area. There were some earthen pots arranged strangely, one above another, in the corner. Curious, I leaned toward them and slowly picked up one after another to check if the amethyst necklace was hidden anywhere. Every single pot was empty. The last one, at the bottom of the pile, had a tiny box inside.

"I opened the box and, to my surprise, it held the amethyst necklace we were looking for. I hid the box in my dress and dashed outside to meet Grandma."

"That was very brave, Liya," said Aisha after hearing about her little sister's encounter.

"After a while, Grandma and I went home, and when you

did not return, we got worried. We realized you were missing, and we have been searching for you the whole day," said Liya, wiping tears from her face, gripped with emotion.

27
THE MYSTERY DEEPENS

AFTER LIYA HAD RECOUNTED ALL the events that helped her find the amethyst, she pulled the box out. "This is the box that I found in Permata's house," said Liya, opening it to reveal the amethyst.

"The only good thing that came out of this is that Shelta's mother is better," said Mother.

"Shelta's mother is still okay?" asked Aisha.

"When you went missing, we walked toward the Bajau tents. There we met Shelta, and she mentioned she had seen you. She said you were heading home," said Mother.

"I went into Shelta's tent to thank her parents for inviting you for dinner the other day, and that is when I saw Shelta's mother had recovered, almost fully."

"How can she be better if the amethyst is back with us?"

"I healed her, my darling. I gave Intan a magic healing potion and asked him to give it to her, even though he didn't believe it would work," said Mother.

"So, he didn't need to steal the amethyst. All he had to do was bring her to you."

"Yes, but he was also greedy for the amethyst. He does not know that it has no value if the person in possession of it is not initiated with healing magic."

"Wait a minute," said Aisha. She hurriedly ran to her bag and opened the worn-out book that Intan had flung out of his tent in anger. "Aha!" she said, flipping through the pages. She stopped at the last entry. "This has the answers to everything."

"What does it say?" asked Mother.

Aisha read from the diary. "'When I was twelve years old, there was a big volcanic eruption at Mount Egon, and everyone was fleeing because of the eruption and the terrible landslide that followed. My little sister was washed away in the flooding river. My mother and I ran around, frantically searching for her.

"'A strange woman had saved my baby sister. I was thankful for that but not what happened after. Overcome by emotion, my mother gave the magical amethyst necklace to her. I will never forget the day I stood helpless, looking at what my mother had done.

"'When I went to get treated, I knew instantly when I saw Zaha wearing the amethyst that it was the same necklace. I have gotten ahold of this magical stone at last, after so many years. My mother didn't even initiate me with magic! She initiated that strange woman's little girl! I will never forget what she did to me, her own son.'"

Aisha, Zaha, and Grandma stared at each other. This story was way too familiar to all of them. "Intan is the Bajau magician's son. No wonder he looked familiar. It's that same moon-shaped scar," said Grandma, breaking the silence.

"I bet his mother did not think he was fit to be a healer. That is why she gave you the amethyst and not him."

"This explains everything. You girls really did a great job. You got the amethyst back and solved the mystery," said Mother.

"Oh no, I still need to get the tiny gems and the diamond. They are still with Permata," said Aisha, starting to head out of the house.

"No, Aisha, you are not going to put yourself in any more danger," Mother said sternly.

Aisha was forced to drop her plan—at least for now. The emerald, ruby, and diamond were still in the house. She worried, *What if the thief strikes again?*

REVELATION

THAT NIGHT, AISHA HAD A very strange dream. She saw the same magician with long, black hair who rose up in a green vapor, calling out to Aisha. This time she was pointing to the lake.

"Put back the four gems, Aisha. You don't have much time left to conquer the dark power. Put them back!"

At the same time, a brown, fiery monster rose up. It was big and powerful, with flames coming out of its mouth.

And then rose Garuda, the magnificent eagle. It pecked at the fiery monster viscously. He then swiftly flew in the direction where the Liang Bua cave was. Perhaps he was angry that the Golden Garuda statue went missing. Aisha ran as fast as she could with the gems, Garuda protecting her along the way. But as she walked over to the lake, she tripped over a huge stone and fell face down on the ground.

Aisha woke up with a start. She noticed she was on the floor. She had fallen face down from her bed. Was this a dream or had the magician just come to her house? As she looked up from her pillow, green vapor wafted out of the window. Aisha pondered, and a thought occurred to her. She had found the answer. She knew where the statue was.

When she walked to the door, she heard someone running and the jingle of anklets. She looked around and saw the shadow of a woman running. It looked like Permata. Aisha looked down at the door, and there was the bag of gems. She quickly opened it—it contained all the tiny gems and the big diamond. Everything was intact. Permata had returned it. *But why?*

Aisha stepped out of the house. She saw a golden hue atop the Kelimutu volcano. She was certain that was Garuda. There was a small commotion. Several townspeople were huddled together and whispering. Yoshi was among them. Aisha patiently waited until everyone disappeared. She ran toward Yoshi.

Aisha quickly shared her dream with Yoshi.

"I have the same feeling that you have, but how could this happen?" said Yoshi. "In my years of sculpting, this has never happened."

The congregation of the bald eagles and the appearance of Golden Garuda had caused quite a stir in their town. Perhaps no one wanted to take their chances or anger Garuda. Aisha hoped she could also find the thieves who broke into the Liang Bua cave to steal the Golden Garuda.

"What about the criminals that tried to steal the statue?

Did you find them?" asked Aisha.

"I had hired two helpers—Suryanto and Darmadiporo—recently to bring supplies and fine tools for chiseling Garuda. They went missing the same day the statue disappeared," said Yoshi. "After seeing Garuda turn alive, they must have run away far to save themselves," said Yoshi, laughing loudly.

"I'm secretly happy that Garuda felt my statue worthy enough to emerge from there," said Yoshi, gazing at his hands.

"You know, you are a really great sculptor," said Aisha, making Yoshi smile sheepishly.

"Now I must run. I have many unfinished tasks," said Aisha as she scurried toward her house.

THINGS GET MORE COMPLEX

AISHA INSPECTED THE BAG THAT Permata had returned again to see the diamond. Permata must have felt guilty and must have decided to return it to the rightful owner. Now that the missing crystals and the four special gems—diamond, ruby, emerald, and amethyst—were in her possession, the next step was for her to find the Garuda statue that the magician had showed her in her dream. She vaguely remembered the location; it was near one of the crater lakes at the peak of Kelimutu. Slowly all the pieces were coming together, except she had never seen a Garuda statue in the mountain. How was she going to find this?

Slowly her mind drifted and she dozed off. Suddenly she heard a tap on her window. The same magician with long, black hair rose up in a green vapor, calling out to Aisha. As Aisha ran toward her, a black storm arose. From behind the dark clouds emerged a gigantic creature. Was it a huge dragon or a bird or a serpent? It had the face of a dragon with a long mouth; instead of ears, huge, gigantic bat wings were attached to the head. It had a long, scaly, serpentine body and a giant, barbed tail that it thumped on the ground when it landed. It let out a huge tumultuous roar. Aisha ran as fast as her legs could carry her until she reached the peak of Kelimutu, but the giant monster was right behind her. Aisha screamed and leapt from the mountain.

Thud! She awoke with a startle on the floor. *What a nightmare,* thought Aisha.

"Not again," said Zaha. "The nightmares are really taking a toll on you. You should stop getting mixed up in these mysteries. This is not child's play."

"But, Mama, we need to find the Garuda statue and put the gems back."

"Maybe, but another day and we need to find a safer way to do it. The two fugitives who tried to steal the Golden Garuda are still around and free, and we are not going to just carry the gems and hope to find the Garuda statue."

"I will think of a better plan, Mama. A foolproof one," said Aisha.

"Not today. You rest now." Zaha tucked Aisha back in bed, leaving Aisha pondering about her next steps.

30
IN SEARCH OF A BETTER PLAN

AFTER AISHA RESTED FOR AN hour, she got up and had breakfast.

At noon she went to Grandma's house. "Mama does not want me to venture out by myself to unite the gems."

"Your mother is right. You are getting yourself mixed up in too many dangerous situations, and you need adult help here."

Aisha shared with Grandma her recent nightmares. She also shared about how the huge Garuda everyone saw in town was the same statue that Yoshi had made.

"Aisha, I fear that you are having visions of the future. If your dream is really going to turn true, then I surely concur with your mother on this. These monsters seem too dangerous. The only one who can truly protect us is Garuda. Seek him out," said Grandma.

Grandma was always right. Perhaps the answer to all this was none other than Garuda. But how could Aisha just seek him out? As she walked out of Grandma's house, a thought occurred to her.

Perhaps Yoshi will know how to seek Garuda.

Aisha walked over to the Moni bus stop. She boarded the bus to the mysterious caves. A lot of things were crossing her mind; she was making several plans in her head, hoping at least one of them would work out. *But will Yoshi agree to her plan?* she thought. She would never know until she asked.

She was determined to share her plans with Yoshi. The bus ride to the mysterious caves seemed longer than the other day. She crossed so many farms and green fields. Several passengers boarded the bus and most of them got off before her stop arrived. She had only two stops left. Suddenly she looked around; there was not a single passenger on the bus. She felt a sudden chill down her spine. She walked over to the front to sit close to the driver. The bus driver was a tall, burly man. He smiled at Aisha.

"Are you going to the mysterious caves alone today?" asked the bus driver, looking concerned.

"I'm looking for Yoshi, I need to talk to him. The matter is very urgent," said Aisha.

"This is my last shift for today. I can come along with you to find him," said the bus driver, offering to help Aisha.

"That is really nice of you. My name is Aisha," she introduced herself.

"My name is Samba," said the bus driver. "I heard about the

Golden Garuda robbery. They must be really daring fugitives," said Samba.

They arrived at the last stop. Since Samba was driving with just Aisha, he rode the bus farther down from the bus stop and close to the mysterious caves. He came to a complete halt near the shade of the tree. He took the keys from the ignition, and they both got off the bus.

THE PLAN

AISHA AND SAMBA WALKED INTO the mysterious caves. They crossed several dark corridors. Aisha heard the shrieking cries of the bats, and several bats flew into the dark tunnels. Aisha held Samba's hand tightly. She was really glad he was with her.

Finally, they reached the place where the Golden Garuda once stood. The scene looked very unfortunate. Piles of rubble and stones had fallen across the ground. The place was very dusty, and a look of gloom was written all across the walls of the caves.

Aisha shared with Samba about the day when she and her mother visited Yoshi, and the look of horror on Yoshi's face when he realized the Golden Garuda was stolen. As they were speaking about the robbery, they suddenly heard a huge creak. Samba pulled Aisha away, and they both hid behind a giant rock.

They heard footsteps. They saw a man with a white *dhoti* and white shawl tug along a small sack. As he tugged the sack, it rumbled against the ground making a loud sound. It looked like there were many metallic objects in the sack, and they were clinking and clanging against each other to make the noise. He finally stopped close to the giant rock where Aisha and Samba were hiding.

He bent and removed something from the sack. It looked like a bell and a gong. He rang the bell. The sound echoed all through the cave, vibrating every stone around. The sound echoed back. The whole cave had a vibrant energy. He then removed the shawl from his head and turned toward where Aisha and Samba hid. Aisha froze and tightly closed her eyes.

"Aisha," said a familiar voice. Aisha opened her eyes. She sighed with a huge sense of relief. It was none other than Yoshi. "You really scared me," said Aisha, hugging Yoshi.

"I saw the bus parked near the tree," said Yoshi. "No one has come near the caves after the robbery. I knew there could be only one daring person who would come this far to see me," said Yoshi with a sparkle in his eyes. "Thanks, Samba, for accompanying her." Yoshi patted Samba.

Yoshi continued, "Tell me, Aisha, what brings you here again?"

"I need to find Garuda. In my dream I saw the Garuda statue on the peaks of Kelimutu," said Aisha anxiously. "I need to unite all the gems. They belong to Garuda, and I need to set them back on his crown," said Aisha. "This is the only way to stop Kelimutu, otherwise we all will perish."

"Are you saying that Golden Garuda has placed the statue on Kelimutu?" asked Yoshi.

"Yoshi, I know my dream is true, the magician cannot lie. She is the spirit of a Bajau woman who gave Mama the amethyst necklace," said Aisha, trying to sound convincing.

Yoshi and Samba looked perplexed, and they looked at each other.

"We need to find the statue on the peak of Kelimutu. I will have to set the four gems on the crown. Garuda will emerge again, Yoshi. He will protect us. He will help me accomplish this goal. He will help me save Moni," said Aisha.

"You have outdone yourself, Aisha," said Yoshi.

"This is a great plan," echoed Samba.

The three of them walked toward the bus and boarded it.

Samba took the driver's seat and Yoshi and Aisha sat together in the first row of the bus.

As Samba reached Moni, Aisha got off the bus. She waved goodbye to Yoshi, and Samba headed to drop Yoshi at the foot of Kelimutu.

IT WAS TIME

AISHA REACHED HOME AND IMMEDIATELY ran to her mother. She told her plan and persuaded her mother to drop everything and join her on the hike up to Kelimutu. "Mama, there is no time to lose. Yoshi is finding the statue of Garuda. We don't know how long the smugglers will remain in hiding at the cave. The fugitives Suryanto and Darmadiporo may try to come back to steal Garuda again. And if Intan realizes we took the amethyst back, he will come after us. And worst of all, Kelimutu may erupt at any time. We have to unite the gems before they get stolen again."

"I agree. Let us quickly take the gems now," said Zaha.

Liya packed the diamond and ruby while Aisha packed her emerald.

"I'm so glad you found the amethyst necklace," said Mother as she fastened it back around her neck.

They started on their ascent to Kelimutu. They climbed the mountain all morning, taking short breaks for snacks.

They finally reached the secret lakes they had discovered on their last trip where they had found their ruby and emerald.

Aisha ran to Tiwu Nua Muri Kooh Tai.

"Let me show you something. Come here," she called out to Liya. As she bent down, she saw her reflection in the water. She was indeed more confident and fearless than she had been the last time they were here. All the mysteries and adventures with the gems had definitely made her more mature. She had a clear mission: she had to save Moni and the townspeople. She had to stop the dark power. She was certain Garuda would help her in this mission.

Aisha removed the emerald from the pouch and bent down to touch the lake. Immediately, a small green glow appeared, and gradually the green color dispersed and spread through the lake, turning the water a sparkling green. Mother and Liya watched this in wonder.

While the lake was shimmering and sparkling, Mother walked toward the shore. "Look at this!"

"The sand has turned into sparkling emeralds!" echoed both Liya and Aisha.

Mother signaled Liya to walk over to Lake Tiwi Ata Mbupu. The water was white in color, but there was no life in the lake. There were no fish. Even the small plants in the lake had dried up again.

"Liya, my girl, this lake needs to be filled with new life," said Zaha. "Please use your healing powers to bring life back to this lake."

Liya took the ruby in her hand, bent down, closed her eyes, and touched the lake.

"I could not be prouder of you both," said Zaha.

"Look at the healthy blue hue in the water," said Aisha. They watched as the lake started bubbling. The dry weeds and plants turned green, and they saw small golden fish, about two to three inches in size, appear. They slowly made their way along in the bubbling water.

Bending down over the water and pointing to the threadfin fish, Mother called out to the girls. "Look at these small fish! This type of fish is very sensitive to changes in the water," she explained. "When the volcano erupted, the water temperature became very high, killing the plankton and the fish."

"You have given new life to them, little sister!" said Aisha.

Mother walked over and kissed Liya's forehead. It was time to return the gems to where they belonged.

33
UNITING THE GEMS

AISHA LOOKED AROUND TO FIND Yoshi. He was nowhere to be seen. She walked up to the third enchanted lake, Tiwu Ata Polo. This lake was red. Liya and her mother walked over to stand next to her. Aisha looked at the serene water. Taking the diamond in her hand, she touched the water.

"Look, Mama, the water is bubbling," said Aisha. There was steam coming out of the hot spring.

"Look, there is something shiny," said Aisha, peering beyond the hot springs. The sunlight revealed a huge statue with a shiny texture that reflected the sunlight.

"We found the Golden Garuda statue!" exclaimed Aisha.

Her mother and Liya stepped into the water to examine Garuda.

Aisha touched the face of Garuda. "Look closely. The crown has four impressions, exactly for the four gems."

Suddenly a gentle hand touched her shoulder. Aisha turned back to see Yoshi. She gave him a tight hug.

"Yoshi, the Garuda is exactly the same as in my dream."

Suddenly dark clouds filled the air. The lake water started bubbling intensely. They saw the fish jump high in the air and fall back. The ground started rumbling, and suddenly there was a tumultuous roar. A huge monster flew in the sky with fire in its mouth. It burned the trees in its path. Soon the entire forest was on fire. Aisha could barely see the monster. It was very smoky, and the air was intense with a pungent odor. Ashes fell from the sky.

Suddenly the monster swooped right past them and landed right in front of Aisha. Liya screamed and rushed to Zaha. Yoshi came running toward Aisha.

The monster looked the same as she saw in her dream. It was humongous. The face resembled a dragon with a long nose. There were no ears; instead, huge bat wings were attached to the head. It had a tapered body like a serpent and a huge, long tail that it swiftly wagged back and forth, breaking and uprooting the trees with its sway. The fiery beast exhaled fire, its breath burning the forest and igniting everything in its path.

Aisha ran as fast as she could through the lake water. The monster continued chasing her. She ran and hugged the Garuda statue. She quickly touched the emerald to the lake water. The lake immediately crystalized, and a green spark flew on the monster. It let out a shrieking cry and stepped away from the lake. Aisha quickly picked some green crystals from the lake and put them in her pockets.

Aisha knew she had only shocked the monster. It would soon return to attack her. She had no time to lose.

"Quick, Mama, Liya, hand over the gems," yelled Aisha. Zaha grabbed Liya's hand and ran toward Aisha.

Suddenly, smoky fumes filled the air. Aisha turned to see that the smoke was coming from Kelimutu. She looked down at Moni. People were already fleeing. Hot molten lava had started pouring down the slopes.

"We should unite the gems for the sake of our town," said Aisha. "We must put the gems into Garuda's crown."

The impressions on the crown looked like a puzzle that had to be completed. It was as if Garuda was calling out to them to hand over their gems. It was time to part ways with the amethyst. It was their only option. With a heavy sigh, Mother removed the amethyst from her necklace and put it in the top-right corner of the crown. She asked Liya to put the ruby in the bottom-right impression on the crown. Liya fit the diamond into another. As Aisha removed her emerald, the monster jumped from nowhere, stopping her in her tracks. As Aisha avoided the monster, she lost her balance and fell—letting go of the emerald. Sadly, she looked down as the emerald fell down the mountain slopes to the bottom. The monster menacingly approached Aisha. By now the top of

Kelimutu had lit up. White wisps of smoke emerged from the peak, growing thicker and stronger. Below, the townspeople continued to flee.

She heard loud screams of "*Gunung Berapi!*" Volcano!

Aisha shrieked, and they watched as the lava poured down the mountain slopes. She could sense the rumbling anger of the dark power. She looked down at her town. *I have to save Moni, my people*, thought Aisha and her sister, feeling even more resolved to conquer the dark power. She had to descend the slopes as fast as possible, but it had taken them such a long time to climb Kelimutu. Aisha chose a very muddy track and tried to slide down the slope as much as she could to increase the speed of her descent. At times they banged into rocks, boulders, and even trees as they slid. Ignoring all the bruises, the sisters made it to the bottom of the slopes. All throughout Aisha was looking for the precious emerald. When she looked back up, her mother was only still halfway down. But there was no time to wait; she ran toward the panic-stricken townsfolk, looking to help them.

"Run! Run as fast as you can. Leave everything behind!" said Grandma, screaming to the townsfolk at the top of her voice.

Why should they leave everything? Maybe they don't need to, thought Aisha. She didn't feel scared or nervous like the others.

I have to save Moni at all costs, thought Aisha, walking

toward the people. As if by sheer luck, Aisha saw the emerald at the bottom stuck to a rock.

"There is nothing to fear," Aisha declared loudly to calm the townsfolk.

Everyone stared at her as if she had lost her mind. Aisha clutched the precious emerald tightly in her hand. She pulled Liya with her and ran to Grandma's house. She was standing outside in shock. They held hands and ran, following the townspeople. They were in great danger, but she could handle this. They just had to get to a safe place.

The townspeople watched as the lava gushed down, hot and sparkling from the mountains. Scared, they ran in all directions. Mother tried to calm them down. As Liya ran fast, she tripped and fell, a jagged rock piercing her knee. Liya started to cry in pain.

Aisha rushed to her side, and a thought occurred to her. If she could control the elements of fire and water, she could surely stop the flowing lava. In desperation, she closed her fingers tightly around the emerald, giving it a squeeze and concentrating all her magic into the one gem. She threw the emerald straight at the flowing lava. As the lava touched the emerald, it solidified and turned into a gleaming rock. Aisha walked toward the rock and picked the emerald.

Then from nowhere again she heard the same tumultuous roar. The monster that had been temporarily stopped swooped through the air and rushed toward Aisha. She held the emerald and waved it in the air frantically.

She had to put it back on Garuda's crown. Aisha had only solidified the flowing lava. This was temporary. She had to stop the volcano. She had to vanquish the monster.

She started to climb the peak of the mountain again, but the monster was right behind her. There was no way she could reach the top. As she began to feel hopeless, a huge, gigantic bird with a golden hue appeared. Garuda emerged and grabbed her, swooping her into the sky. He flew her high into the clouds. The monster was shrieking while flying and chasing Garuda. The golden eagle was too fast for the monster. He flew fast, circling around Kelimutu in high intensity. Aisha closed her eyes, holding the emerald in one hand and Garuda's neck tightly in the other hand.

Golden Garuda gracefully flew to the lake and perched down next to the statue. Aisha rushed and waded into the lake. As she was reaching to put the emerald into the crown, the monster let out a menacing bellow. Aisha ignored it and thrust the emerald in the last impression on the crown. Immediately the monster let out a thunderous roar of agony. Aisha watched as a bolt of lightning from the clouds struck it with blinding force, hurling it down the mountainside in a fiery spiral. The beast convulsed and twitched, its scales charred and its body was smoking. The monster was electrocuted and that was the end of it.

In an instant, the smoke covering Kelimutu disappeared. The volcano stopped fuming and slowly calmed down.

Aisha walked toward the majestic Garuda. She bowed her head down to Garuda's feet. The giant majestic bird raised its two wings to signal victory to Aisha.

Liya and Zaha ran toward Garuda, rejoicing.

Aisha had stopped the volcano with her determination. She had saved Moni. She had saved her people. She was a true hero. She wasn't a cursed child after all. Aisha climbed over Garuda and signaled her mother and Liya to join her. Garuda majestically flew through the sky around Kelimutu and brought them down the slope. All the townspeople gathered around Aisha and Liya. Grandma joined her hands and prayed up to the stars as if thanking them.

This was a moment Aisha had imagined, about a million times in her head. Instead of fear in the eyes of the townspeople, she saw love and affection. Kids were smiling at her instead of flinching. The same little girl that had yelled at Aisha and had told her to leave the town came running toward her. Aisha knelt down on her knee and held the little girl with open arms.

Garuda flew up in the sky and said, "Aisha, you are special. Your family was gifted with magic due to the kindness of your grandmother. You truly care for the people in the town, and the town needs your family. Your town is safe now that you have subdued the dark power. But soon outsiders will come back to learn the secret of the mysterious gems. Guard them with your life."

Yes, she would guard the Garuda statue and gems at all costs. There would be no more danger to Moni, her town. She would, as the chosen savior, protect her people.

Suddenly there was lightning and thunder, followed by a brief rain shower. As the rain pitter-pattered on the rocks and the mountains, the fumes from Kelimutu died down. It looked majestic and serene again. Aisha had saved the town. She had done it!

The waterfall looked magical as it splashed over the giant, jagged rocks. It was hard to believe the cascading falls could create such a calm pool at the bottom. Aisha looked around. Her family knew what she was thinking. Aisha jumped into the pool, followed by Liya.

As Aisha and her family sat on the ground watching the light rain stop, Aisha remembered she still had one last task: to find the smugglers and return their loot to its rightful owners.

Aisha looked at the smugglers' cave. There was no way they had enough time to cross over the mountain to get there. She would have to use her magic to outwit the smugglers. She had to use elemental power.

I need to somehow trick the smugglers that the volcano is erupting without making the townspeople panic, thought Aisha. She focused intently on the smugglers' cave on the far side of the mountain. Through her power, smoky fumes emerged from the cave entrance.

"Look, Aisha, the smugglers are rushing out of the cave." Liya laughed. "They think these are smoky fumes from the volcano. They are running for their lives! Great job, Aisha!"

Indeed, the smugglers were running as fast as they could, not even trying to take any of their stolen loot.

"They will not return if they know what's good for them," said Mother. "I will get the townspeople to help remove the stolen goods and return them to their rightful owners."

THE END

AISHA STILL COULD NOT QUITE believe the last month. She'd discovered her powers and her destiny and helped save Moni and her townspeople. Although she'd subdued the dark power, Intan's anger and the wrath of the smugglers were ongoing problems, as was anyone who might hold a vengeance against her when they realized their loot was gone.

Suddenly, her thoughts were broken when Liya called out to her, "Aisha, the Bajaus are leaving."

Aisha turned. It was true. They were dismantling their tents and putting all their belongings into their rugged canoes and plank boats. All the Bajaus were hurriedly heading back to the boats with their possessions, and their children were following them.

"The Bajau people are nomadic. They do not stay in one place. They are great masters of the sea," Mother reminded Aisha and Liya.

"They barely stayed here a month."

"You have had your share of adventure this month, chasing after them for your gems," said Grandma.

Aisha noticed that Liya looked sad. They watched all the Bajaus board their boats—with the exception of two people. Shelta and her mother stood looking in their direction.

"Aisha, Liya, it looks like Shelta and her mother have something to say to us. Let's go say goodbye," said Mother. The three walked toward Shelta and her mother.

Shelta's mother had a healthy glow on her face. "I could not leave without thanking you and your lovely girls."

"I will never forget you," said Shelta, tearing up and hugging Aisha and Liya.

"We will miss you too, Shelta. You have been a great friend," said Aisha. "I hope you come back and visit us."

As they were leaving, Shelta's mother handed Zaha a small basket. "I wanted to give this to you for all that you and your girls have done for me and our family."

Mother took the woven basket. It was really lovely.

"I'm truly sorry for what Intan did. I hope you can forgive him," continued Shelta's mother.

"Yes, I know he meant no harm. It was an old grievance he was holding on to. Let's put it behind us."

Aisha and Liya walked up to Shelta and handed her a small bag. Shelta opened the bag to see a ring studded with two pearls, colored white and pink and surrounded by tiny, colorful gems. "This is so beautiful," said Shelta, looking closely at the ring the sisters had made for her. "Aren't these the same pearls I found for both of you when we swam and dove together?"

The tiny gems around the ring shone in the sunlight.

"You are really special, Shelta. We will cherish your friendship," said Aisha.

With tears in her eyes, Shelta gave Aisha and Liya a big hug. With that, Aisha and Liya bid Shelta and her mother a fond farewell. They watched until the last boat had floated from view, and then they turned to head back home.

THE END

ACKNOWLEDGEMENTS

I THANK JESS COHN, GILLIAN Barth, and the entire Mascot Books publishing team for helping me bring this book out to the world. I also thank the JV Graphic Design team for the amazing cover art and illustrations.

ABOUT THE AUTHOR

 **HAMSA BUVARAGHAN IS AN INDO-CANADIAN** residing in Bay Area, California, with her husband and two daughters. The idea for her book spawned from her experiences with Indonesian children when she volunteered with a nonprofit called Indonesia Street Children Organization. She writes multicultural fantasy novels that explore themes of racial diversity, courage, family, and friendship. Hamsa is a technology leader at Google and also writes business technology books. She holds a Master of Business Administration with honors in global management and a Bachelor of Engineering in computer science.

hamsabuvaraghan.com

ABOUT THE COAUTHORS

RIYA IS A SIXTH GRADER residing in Bay Area, California. Her interests include creative writing, piano (level 7), karate, and basketball. In her free time, she tinkers with STEM projects.

EESHA IS A JUNIOR HIGH school student residing in Bay Area, California, currently studying for her IB Diploma. She holds a black belt in martial arts. Her other interests include music (piano, level 10), creative writing, and theatre. She is interested in pursuing biomedical engineering and pre-medicine.